I0739919

# Samsara

## Wolf Howling

**Samsara: Wolf Howling**

Copyright © 2018 by Brian Van Brunt

All rights reserved. No part of this book may be reproduced, distributed, or transmitted in any printed or electronic form, without the prior written permission of the author, except for certain non-commercial uses permitted by copyright law. For permission requests, contact the publisher, Light Rising Publishing.

**Disclaimer**

This is a work of fiction. Names, characters, businesses, products, places, events, locales, and incidents are either the products of the author's imagination or used in a fictitious manner. Any resemblance to actual persons, living or dead, or actual events is purely coincidental.


**Acknowledgements**

My deepest thanks to Cynthia and Jon for coming to my rescue with layout, the audiobook, and Web design. To Melissa, Sarah, Lara, Bethany, and Amy; your edits and suggestions helped make this book a better project. Also to Melissa, thank you for your edits and timeless advice on stabbing murder practices.

**Light Rising Publishing**
www.lightrisingpublishing.com

**Design & Layout**
Cynthia E. Gomez
Light Rising Publishing

**Cover**
Original cover painting "Black Cat in Alley" by Sean Friloux
www.seanfriloux.com
Cover design by Austin Albany

**Photos**
Brian Van Brunt

**Illustrations**
"Side-Eye Rabbit" and "Cassandra's Neck" by Bethany Van Brunt
"What Big Teeth You Have" by Emily Van Brunt
Margin Art by Emily and Bethany Van Brunt

ISBN 978-1-7328238-0-8

Printed in the United States of America.

This book contains mature themes, descriptions of graphic violence, sexual content, and harsh language. Reader discretion is advised.

# Dusk

# Chapter 1
## New Orleans, Spring, Tuesday 4:45ᵖᵐ

She finally found him, sitting on the curb in front of Rouses Market. He had eluded her for a long time. She knew he had a few regular spots and was checking those first, amongst the rabble of the Quarter. Sinclair was a creature of habit and this fact made her life easier. She strolled by his apartment and saw his cat; she knew from past visits if Faulkner was in the window, Sinclair was not in the apartment. His furry little familiar stuck by his side when he was home.

She wore a tank top with a lightweight brown linen chemise and dust colored tights. Her dirty blonde hair was tied back in a mixture of dreadlocks and a tangle of waves. She blended into the city; at a glance, she was just another homeless street kid passing down Decatur in the early summer heat of the Big Easy.

One time, she had found Sinclair inside a bar on Frenchman Street. He was listening to jazz while sipping a gin and tonic with too many limes, as always. She remembered laughing at that; he was like some kind of pirate in danger of catching scurvy. Him and those limes. Twice, she found him spinning back and forth on a diner stool of the Crescent City Grille at the low end of Bourbon. Another handful of times, she found him in the back of the Jackson Square Cathedral. Yet today, he wasn't in any of these places.

She knew him well. She had spent time following him. It was part of her assignment. She knew Sinclair lost himself in music and drinking, those infamous distractions of the city. Which was why the two of them had been at this for so long. His lack of focus.

She tugged at Oliver, her big, speckled, hound dog, as he trailed behind her. He sniffed a bit too long at some unknown bit of trash on the sidewalk. She pulled on the worn rope leash and he came to her side. Her outfit and dog fit the motif of the city. They both blended in, as she was required to do. Just part of the gig.

She crossed down Saint Ann on the way to Bourbon. Colorful rainbow flags hung at the end of the street against a backdrop of flickering gas lamps outside the Hotel de Lion. She turned left onto Bourbon and walked past Paradise Lost. No Sinclair today. She knew this was another favorite spot of his. Probably because of the blonde, large-chested bartender. Yet another one of Sinclair's problems. He was drawn to distraction at every turn; this trifecta of music, women, and booze. She had this fear he would never figure things out. She sighed and continued down Bourbon to St. Peter's. Then she had a sudden inspiration and tugged at Oliver's rope, leading him to another spot where he might be.

She followed her hunch and thought about the last time she lost him for so long. She had finally found him in the old church, Our Lady of Guadalupe. He was in the shrine at the back; just sitting there and looking at the flames of the candles. God damn tortured artists. They were exhausting.

She was tired, bone tired, and was more than ready to move onto her next assignment; she was weary of Sinclair. On top of that, the heat and humidity of this modern-day Sodom and Gomorrah had lost any brief charm it had once held. This made his lack of motivation and direction drain her even more.

She turned the corner and saw him. Of course, here he was.  He sat on the curb like a damn homeless person. She sighed again and made an unpleasant comment under her breath about tortured artists. Maybe her next assignment would be someone a little more exciting, or at least in a better climate. Anyway, time to get this going. Oliver sat down obediently at her side. She knelt behind Sinclair.

*And it began again.*

# Chapter 2
## New Orleans, Spring, Tuesday, 4:45ᵖᵐ

found the note when I woke up at one o'clock in the afternoon. I know, I know, it's the afternoon; but I slept in. I do that sometimes. Don't be a fuck about it.

I'm at my desk in Monroe Hall overlooking the university quad. Outside, the campus is green and bright, full of cypress trees. It's a warm spring day. I look at the trees closely and I can't be sure; the movement is difficult to see from this far away. It probably isn't them. Not this time…probably. Valentine and Mr. Conrad aren't around.

I found the folded sheet of paper tucked underneath my door; she must have left it for me sometime early in the morning. Like the bitch had some right to come to my door after I went to sleep. She just slid it underneath like it didn't matter. Which, of course, is the problem really; that it didn't matter, not to her. I didn't matter. Not to that fucking bitch. Not anymore. Probably not ever, now that I think about it.

See. But I do matter. She should know that. I'll make her see that. But I'm getting ahead of myself. I do that sometimes. Just stay with me. It's not that hard. Don't be a fuck about it. My next class is the History and Systems of Psychology. It starts in twenty minutes. I won't be attending. Not today. Today is a special day. That fucking bitch made it a special day. Yes, she did.

I read the note, again. My 'Dear John' letter, if you will. That's just a figure of speech, you know. Because my name is not John. My name is Albert. Not even close to John. Anyway, I finish reading it and I start over again. It's short, 100 words exactly. "I treated you bad." Well, at least she got that part correct. But the goddamn hubris of her to write this. I read it once more and then I go away. I disappear for bit. When I come back, the note is all ripped up. Just scattered bits of paper on my desk. Which, if I am being honest with you, is a surprise. My desk looks like a goddamn mess of confetti, like someone had a parade. But there isn't a parade today. And I don't remember how it got ripped up. That happens sometimes.

The paper bits litter my otherwise SPECTACULARLY clean desk. I write that word in all CAPS for emphasis. Just for you. You should know this about me—I like to keep things clean and in order. The world is fucked up enough, so this really is the least I can do. Take a fucking minute or two and do things the way they are supposed to be done. It's not so hard with the right dedication; the right sense of purpose. It's right there in *The Book of Albert*. Chapter 1:2, "Preparation, after all, is the first commandment." Too bad most people don't take the time anymore. America ain't so great again after all, is it?

Amid the ripped paper, a single word is visible, not completely torn like the rest of the mess. Just one word and it looks up at me. The word is RIGHT. She made it all lowercase, but I put it in all CAPS here, again for emphasis. Just for you, so you know it's important. I want you to see what a goddamn fucking whore writes like. I want you to understand what happens next. How she lit the fuse. How she primed my pump. Right? RIGHT.

My fingers find some solace as I reach for the hardwood stick I keep next to my desk. I set it across my lap. It's slightly thinner than a broom handle, but just as long. I find the wood soothing as my fingers tighten around it. I've had it for a long time. We've seen some action together, the stick and me. Mr. Conrad has gotten a smack or two over the years, that beady-eyed mother-fucker. Valentine, not so much. That cunt gives me the willies.

Anyway, as I was saying, there's a loyalty between the stick and me. Like Excalibur for Lancelot, Santiago to the old man. It's a deeper commitment, spanning decades. Unlike how long that bitch Olivia lasted. I had her for two months. I've had my stick for much longer than that.

And listen, you have to know her name. That's why I said it. I won't say it again. I won't give her the satisfaction. I have a new sound for her name now. I prefer BITCH and FUCKING WHORE. But that can get confusing. So here you are. My narrative device to you. I told you her given name. End of the last paragraph. You can read it again if you forgot. I won't say it again. I'm trying to not be a fuck about it, I just thought you should know. Let's move on.

I sweep the torn paper into the trashcan and make a mental note to empty it later. I don't like a mess, even in the trashcan. There's a pile of books organized by ascending size stacked neatly at the corner of my desk. That's how I like to do it. It's ordered that way and soothes me some. A flyer for Pirate Alley Ghost Tours sits tucked between the books and the lamp. I allow it to be there because it has significance, an exception to the rule, if you will. On the top of the book pile is my favorite book. It's small, with a red and black cover, and is face down. I can see Mr. Sinclair's face staring up at me from the back material.

I rest the stick on my lap and pick up the book. I like the way it feels in my hands. Firm and soothing. Reassuring whispers. Words like "BESTSELLER" and "NEW YORK TIMES LIST 10 Weeks Running!" are on the front cover. If I'm being honest with you, I'm still mad at myself for reading it so fast the first time. Just took the whole thing in one big gulp. I didn't know. I should have savored it; relished it. But I just took it all at once, skipping Professor Carter's Introduction to Sociology to read it. No big loss, though; not like I missed the class. I say this out loud to my empty room, "Well, I wouldn't say I was missing it, Bob."

That's from a movie I like. I'm telling you this because sometimes I get thinking so fast I lose people that I'm engaged with. And I'm engaged with you, aren't I? It's important for an author to engage their reader. I don't want to lose people, so I slow down. This allows them to keep up. They say some fish never stop swimming. Just always moving through the water. My mind is like that. Always moving and never at rest. Listen, don't be a fuck about it. It's just the way I am.

Sinclair's book is an inspiration to me. More than that really. It's my goddamn Mecca. My own personal Jesus. I'm not sure why it took me so long to find my path, to see my compass swing true north, but when I read that book, I knew. It gave me a sense of purpose. All my suffering suddenly had meaning, things came into focus.

Like it says in Chapter 5:13, "Travel in my footprints on the beach; I shall carry you and you will never be forsaken." Reading Sinclair's book was like reading the note the BITCH slid all sneaky-snakey under my door. I went away for a little bit and came back with this spark of inspiration. I had the most fascinating ideas. The book helped me assemble the bomb; that BITCH lit the fuse. I set the book back, facedown, on the pile where it goes.

I'm laughing now. I feel like that is important for you to know. It's an unsettling low chuckle. It's 'cause I'm thinking about that movie again. No, I wouldn't miss attending class today, no sir. How much could I miss it, really? You should understand that as well. Everything at this school is dumbed down for the good ol' boy network. Fraternity keggers and playing football gives those special few a green wave of privilege into cushy jobs around Louisiana. I'll be fine catching up. Probably could teach the class if I needed to.

I pick up the stick again and tap it on the floor and think about that BITCH. I can't believe that goddamn snatch thinks she can just end it with me. Tap. Tap. Tap. She just thinks it's as easy as breaking up through a ridiculous Dear John letter? I'm Albert, bitch. Tap. Tap. Tap. She knows that. I find this entire day unsettling. Though, it's unsettling in this kind of apocalypse meets the rapture way. I'm not sure if you can understand, but that's how I'm feeling. Like I'm shedding something and there is this bright, white-hot peace underneath it all. Like burning bush shit. Swallowed by a whale. I'm on a journey and I'm sliding down the chute pretty damn fast.

I put the stick down and place both my hands across the smooth, clean desk. It's been built for sturdiness and longevity. I can feel my thoughts moving in the water. Sleek and legion. They do that sometimes. When it happens, the smoothness of the wood calms me down some. All part of the larger plan. And with this BITCH, it's not like I hadn't expected it. She was recruited like the others. Sly bitch. Black goth-haired, sly bitch with saggy tits already at nineteen. Who has saggy tits at nineteen? The first time she took off her bra, they just sagged down. And that's what my erection did as well, I'll tell you that. And you should know this as well, she was a drunk. A fucking drunk. And really that's part of the problem, isn't it? Just a total lack of goddamn dedication to anything. A lack of INTENTIONALITY.

Except writing that note. That was one thing she apparently had no fucking compunctions about. Setting pen to paper for my little fucking treat. Slipping it under my door like some kind of sneaky snatch snake. I like that alliteration. Sneaky Snatch Snake. That is her to a goddamn T. Eve munching on that apple started the whole machine in motion.

Did you know it wasn't an apple? It doesn't say that anywhere. People are these fucking retarded lemmings just following  the herd. Could have been a tomato or fucking banana. But apple is our collective delusion. Another example of the collective shit people swallow and then ask for more with a stupid grin on their faces. Mindless sheep, the whole lot of them. Mindless. Fucking. Sheep.

I'm getting worked up. I can feel my needle going into the red. I need to keep my cool. I pick up the stick. It's calming as I touch it. Bells ring outside from the tower on the quad. I trace the number nineteen on my desk with my finger. You won't understand that, so I won't even try to explain it to you. It's about the bells and the tower. But what I'm about now is Ms. Saggy Tits. Ms. Sneaky Snatch Snake.

And listen, I don't want you to get this wrong; I am not some worthless pile of shit feeling sorry for myself. There is no doubt I'm better off without this BITCH pulling me down to her level of feminine foolishness and folly. She was never worth my time. She meant nothing to me. Means nothing. Drunk fucking WHORE.

Yet…yet….there's a balance that has been unsettled. And this will not do. There needs to be a reckoning to set things right.

I wonder how much she knows about them. If Valentine and Mr. Conrad told her to tempt me and tease me. To draw me to the bait and then YANK. It's how they work, waiting until I needed her the most, until that point when I finally considered feeling something for the BITCH. That's when Valentine's hook was set, piercing me. This is exactly the kind of bullshit the Sneaky Snatch Snake would engage in with me. God-damn puppet of the sharks.

But the joke is on her, right? Because I always held a little back; a little in reserve. Best to keep it that way. Best to always keep a little in the reserve tank. Slipped that damn hook.

So, history lesson time. I don't think you will understand all of this, but I'm trying to give you some context. Don't be like all those fucking millennial masses out there who can't focus for one single goddamned minute. This helps build the arc. Helps you understand some. Don't be a fuck about it and just keep reading.

My father was a mean drunk. He used to joke with me about sharks in the bathtub. That's where this all started. The bastard must have thought it was funny at the time. Between you and me, I think it's fair to say that I disagreed vehemently with that particular assessment of that fucker, my father Lou. He would turn off the bathroom lights and hum the *Jaws* music. Just to add a little dash to the mix. Just to make the terror rise to the point of Cthulhu. Insanity and chaos in a swarming mass of darkness. Did I mention I was five at the time? Father of the year, Lou was.

The prick's mean streak was only out-shadowed by his creativity. One of the fucker's gifts, I suppose. Lou was always able to come up with better ways to scare me when he had been drinking. Once, he actually opened a can of tuna fish and put it behind the toilet. I remember that particular bath in vivid detail. The whole place smelling like fish. My fear oily and dark as it rose to a fever pitch.

At first, I would scream. I'd scream with all I could muster. That didn't help. My mother worked double shifts like Chinamen ate rice, as that prick Lou would say. So, she wasn't there. And good old Lou? Well, I think he liked it when I screamed like that. I think he got off on it. So I learned to just keep it all inside. Not to give him that satisfaction. But at first? Well, yes, I screamed. Screamed like I was on fire.

Hey.  Don't you be a fuck about this. Don't start feeling sorry for me. I'm fine. You just need to know this because this is important. This is how I first learned about them, Valentine and Mr. Conrad. I'm not gonna make Lou out to be some kind of midwife to my terrors, but he goddamn well unlocked the door that showed them the way. The same as Sinclair. Well, not the same. Sinclair showed me what was in the light; Lou just gave birth to Valentine and Mr. Conrad.

At this point in the story, you should know that all this fucked with me. This shark shit with Lou. I know that. I'm not unaware. I should have cracked Lou over his drunken fucking head with the hardwood stretched out right here on my lap. But I didn't. I was just a kid. It wasn't the time for action. The bomb was charging, but the fuse hadn't been lit yet. But that didn't stop me from thinking about it.

If I'm being honest with you, sure as fuck I dream about going back in time Marty McFly-style and walking up to my old man and just cracking open his goddamn skull. I smile when I see the crimson in my mind. The look of surprise on my old man's face when the staff makes contact. I can even hear the crack of wood meeting bone. I have a good imagination. Casey wouldn't miss this time. Takes the first pitch dead on and pops up a strong fly ball to right field. Going, going…gone.

Alright, alright; I didn't hit my father, but the desire was certainly there. And I know what they say about desire. 90 percent inspiration and 10 percent perspiration. Something like that. And I'm feeling inspired today. Inspired to cut those saggy tits off that curly haired Sneaky Snatch Snake. She will pay for her disrespect. This is about that. Telling you about the reckoning that is coming.

You also should know this part. When I was eight, the shit started getting real. Those sharks were everywhere. Big razor-sharp teeth, grey oily skin, black beady eyes. They spoke to me in a raspy voice. A trench coat and dark sunglasses voice. "Hey, kid. Come over here." Old-time gangster. Straight up, dirty glass, whiskey-gravel voice. I heard these voices often. Fucking Greek chorus that followed me around. This was before Valentine and Mr. Conrad showed up. The early years, if you will.

The sharks lived in the trees; that's where they usually stayed. They liked the tall oak trees with lots of thick green leaves. I don't know why the trees appealed to the sharks. Maybe the rustling of the leaves disguised their voices. Maybe it was the height. I can tell you this though, they sure as shit loved dropping down from above. They would land with this meaty thud. This wet sound of their leathery skin hitting the concrete. I can still hear it when I close my eyes. I think they did it because it gave them the element of surprise. They brought that with them when they came ashore. Dragged it out of the ocean with them from the depths. Swarming dark masses swimming up from beneath to hunt their prey.

When I was walking to school, I found a certain path to avoid the sharks. I mean, I was terrified, right? I was just a little shit and I had better figure out a way around this or I was going to lose my goddamn mind, right? Those beady eyes and gravelly voices fucked with me something fierce. Snapping, biting teeth. "Hey, kid." With a slap of their tail they said, "C'mere." Fuck that. I ran fast down that path and avoided oak trees on the way to school. But the running wouldn't work. I knew running was careless. People could see me. Peering out at me like minnow fish watching the predator after its prey. I learned to be careful about what people could see and what they should not see. Subterfuge. It wasn't an easy lesson, but it was one I took to heart.

Oh, another thing. I had a little brother, once upon a time. His name was Joe. It's important for you to know this because his sandbox was another place where the sharks would hide, those sneaky fuckers. Before all of this shit started with Lou, I used to stage elaborate Lego battles between Harry Potter and his friends against Voldemort and the death eaters. It was one of the fond memories of my childhood. One of the few, a time when I was left alone.

But then, those fuckers, they began to swim beneath the sand. When the sand was smooth, I knew the sharks were not there. So, I figured if I could smooth the sand with the upside-down part of the broken rake my father kept in the garage, I could outsmart these fuckers. Long strokes, over and over. It generally took an hour to get the sand to an acceptable level of smoothness. First horizontal and then vertical. I would watch for the occasional disturbance from beneath. I knew the sharks were sneaky, intelligent and hungry. Any slip in the routine could lead to a missing finger or, if they got a good grip on me, I could have ended up right in the middle of the sandbox. It would have been a fucking feeding frenzy.

It was the worst in the winter. The sharks didn't like the cold and moved indoors. Not that it ever got too cold. Not in Baker, Louisiana. They had this particular affinity for kitchen cabinets. The sharks got thinner and longer in the winter. Hungrier. Like they had stored up their fat and slowly worked through it over the cold months. Their raspy voices became whispers. More reptilian. Thinner, but just as angry. And their teeth; well, those bright white serrated fuckers looked just as sharp.

This is when I got my stick. It was a wooden dowel crafted from something sturdy, like oak or walnut. I first saw it in the corner at my Cub Scout den meeting. Not that my parents had anything to do with me attending the Cub Scouts. It was an afterschool program I signed up for myself to spend less time at home with my parents and brother. At the meeting, they hoisted the felt flags on these poles as the scouts recited the pledge of allegiance and the Cub Scout motto. Bullshit patriotic indoctrination, but I wasn't thinking about that at the time. I was thinking about the dowel. It was the perfect size, two inches thick and four feet long.

I snuck it out of the meeting one week and into my mother's car during snack time. This time was particularly well suited for distraction, as the other scouts were focused on the orange flavored drink and sugar cookies the den mother cautiously distributed in a manner that would have made the staunchest Marxist proud. Mom was chatting it up with the other parents outside the school and smoking unfiltered camels like some kind of fucking truck driver from Alabama.

The stick fit perfectly under the passenger seat. There was something about the shape that intrigued me. I first thought of just taking a broomstick handle but really, my parents would have noticed that. Probably not my mom—that bitch wasn't around. But Lou? Oh, you better believe Lou would have tuned into that channel. Watched it all night long. And then I would also have to explain the teeth marks.

Unacceptable. My battle with the sharks was to be a private matter. Any attempt to bring my concerns to the outside world would have been met with increasingly vicious attacks from the sharks. So, it was just between us.

I kept the stick under my bed until I needed something from the kitchen cabinets. Mom worked as a nurse in Baton Rouge; I'd guess she wanted time away from Lou and his drinking as much as I did. Although, this meant I had to forage for my own breakfast.

I woke up early before anyone else and used the stick to push open the high cabinet next to the refrigerator. The sharks usually got one or two chomps on the stick before I was able to knock the box of Honeycombs free. "Hey, kid. Cut it out. Kid." Their voices were gravelly and drawn-out, "Give me the stick, kiiiiiiiiiiiiid!"

The box, more often than not, fell and spilled its contents across the kitchen counter. I gathered the spilled Honeycombs while the sharks watched me with their oily skin and hungry eyes. I can still hear them, "C'mere kid. We won't hurt ya." Sure, right. Never trust a shark.

I took a few pieces of sandpaper from school and polished the stick clean in my room at night. I used some leftover stain from a project Joe had at school to give the stick a dark sheen. I liked the routine and consistency of the process. It also smoothed out the bite marks. That kind of repetitive action calmed me. Like with my journal. But I'll get to that later.

It was a particularly unlucky Thursday morning when my father found the stick under my bed. It ended up, as with many assorted objects, in the back of Lou's pickup truck. "I took that pole of yours. Need it to get the mud clear from under the wheel wells." He told me this absentmindedly, like it didn't even matter at all.

I remember trying to keep the panic out of my voice. "But that's mine. I found it."

"You don't need the damn stick. Leave it alone, you hear?" he answered.

I didn't have a choice. I'd have my time with the stick again but for now, I left it alone. I was able to avoid the cabinets for a week or so before the sharks got angry. They wouldn't let me just walk away. That's not how the battle was fought. At night, I heard them as they slithered about the house. I could hear them propel their leathery skin across the hardwood floors. It made a wet pulling sound, like damp newspaper dragged across a sidewalk.

"Hey kid" came the voice from the hall. I'd turn on the TV in the morning to drown them out. Get it? Drown them. But Mom wanted to know who had gotten up and turned it on. I blamed Joe. I told Mom that I saw Joe sleepwalking. Joe didn't see the sharks, so I figured this was a fair exchange for him. Why should he get a free pass? Ridiculous. If Joe couldn't see the sharks, at the very least he should be dragged off to the neurologist to talk about his nocturnal appliance usage. That's how I saw it.

Meanwhile, the sharks found a new place to roam. They began splashing and circling about in the toilet. And listen, don't be a fuck about this. I know you're going to judge me, but I'd like to see you do better. I started pissing the bed in the middle of the night. I tried to hold it in and just use the bathroom at school, but sometimes I just couldn't. I'd like to see what you would have done. Those sharp teeth waiting. Sometimes I would keep a bottle in there and then empty it. But having Lou find a bottle of piss in my room would have ended with a beating. So, I tried to hold it. It didn't always work.

And then there were the weekends. No school. No safe bathroom. Did you think of that? I didn't think so. It was a losing battle, falling asleep dreaming of rushing rivers and booming waterfalls. But I would be goddamned if I would use that toilet. They talked to me in there. "Come use the john, kid. I'll bite it off. A little snack to tide me over till something more substantial comes along."

And let me tell you, a twelve-year-old who wets his bed is not received well by a distant, workaholic mother who hates doing the laundry. It's received even worse by an abusive, mean drunk of a father always on a hair trigger. Mom was less and less pleased with my wetting problems and Joe's nighttime wandering. Lou started hitting me so hard he left bruises on my arms and lower back. It didn't take much to set him off. Maybe you know the type. I did.

One night, Lou woke up at 3am to the sound of hammering in the kitchen. He turned on the lights and found me pounding nails into the kitchen cabinets with the hammer. And, of course, the sharks were all quiet when Lou flipped on the kitchen light. Of course. Sneaky fuckers.

"What the god-damn hell..." was all I heard before Lou knocked me to the ground and gave me a fierce beating. "You'll remember this, you little piece of shit!"

The next morning, my mother dragged me to the first meeting with the school counselor. I remembered the way my mother looked at me as she sat next to me. All worry and concern.

The BITCH should be worried. She sold me out. She told them all about my bed-wetting, late night television watching, combing the sandbox for hours with a rake, talking to myself, and putting nails in the cabinets. She used fancy nurse words like Autism and Obsessive-Compulsive Disorder. I could only imagine what she would have said if she knew about the sharks. But for me, it didn't matter. By then, the sharks had gone underground, hiding somewhere else, plotting and planning, preparing their two emissaries.

Which, in some ways, was worse. I knew what paranoid was. How it was defined. I had the Internet. But I also knew that people couldn't be trusted. I saw how they washed their hands. The piss-poor way they cleaned up after themselves. I knew how lazy and stupid they were. How they did everything with the very least amount of effort. I knew they weren't on my level from a young age; they certainly should not be trusted in any significant way.

I learned at the university not to talk about the sharks; I kept these thoughts to myself. During my freshman year, I had been forced to meet with a psychologist after I had an "outburst" in class. That's what they called it—an outburst. An unacceptable outburst interrupting the academic learning environment. I had seen Valentine for the first time and I think my reaction was rather reasonable. Intense, lengthy screams.

The psychologist I met with went to the gym too much. He reminded me of Vin Diesel, with his bald head and those disconcerting veins. Like they were ready at any moment to come crashing through his skin. I disliked him immediately, the way he shook my hand and then wiped his nose. The way the stack of books and papers on his desk was haphazardly piled without respect to size or color. And the staleness of the office, like you could smell the pathetic sadness of the last person he talked to hanging in the air. It was safe to say I didn't care for Dr. Robert Hawkins in the least.

And while I didn't like him, I already told you fuckers that I'm not stupid. I'm smart enough to be aware of the power Vin Diesel held over me. The fear hung in the air like the smell of a skunk days after it had sprayed someone. I told Vin Diesel about the sharks. Cautiously at first; I was no fool, but I was worried. I just told him the basics.

Hell, if I had it together I wouldn't have shouted about the sharks in class to begin with. That's what caused this whole mess.

So that small moment of weakness with Vin Diesel, the mentioning of the sharks in the trees around campus, was enough to cause the psychologist to watch me. Like something out of Orwell's *1984*. Big Brother was watching me. I knew I had to be on good behavior.

They called my father. He couldn't be bothered to come to campus. The embarrassment of them calling my father was something that stuck with me like a violation. Vin Diesel treated me like a child and I was no child. No. They'll all see that. It's best not to underestimate me.

I'm sure if my mother was there, smelling of smoke and hospital disinfectant, she would have had something to say. Her petite self, brimming with that superficial southern charm. "Yes, Dean? Oh, my! I'm sure he didn't say such a thing." Just like middle school all over again. But she wasn't there. The cancer took her right before Valentine showed up. And listen, don't be a fuck about it. I'm fine. Better off without her and Lou. Parents of the fucking year.

The take-away from my time at Counseling and Psychological Services was simple. I don't talk about the sharks anymore with anyone. I told Vin Diesel I was not a danger to others or myself. I met with him three more times and was successful in convincing him that I was not going to cause any more problems.

That was last year. I had agreed to meet with a psychiatrist to consider medications. I was smart and dedicated enough to sit quietly and listen to the psychiatrist, a fat man who moved as slow as the hot New Orleans summer heat. The sweat pouring off his head was just as disgusting as the armpit stains under his ill-fitting oxford shirt.

He had a mess of a desk, with a prescription pad haphazardly lying next to a pile of charts and unanswered phone messages. And a partially used napkin on the desk next to his half-finished lunch; the smell of Pad Thai still lingering in the office. Why would I listen to a man who was so clearly not only a disaster of a human being, but also in league with the others plotting against me? Maybe that was part of their ruse. Giving me a sloth of a psychiatrist to try get me to let my guard down.

It's one of my most strongly held pet peeves, my Achilles heel, if you will. You should know that about me. A lack of dedication and commitment. Lazy and unfocused people. That's really the problem with our society. People lost staring off into the TV and Facebook. No one lives life intentionally anymore. I do. When I see something, I go for it. Laser focused. I just hadn't found something yet to focus on. Not until Mr. Sinclair gave me some guidance. Showed me the light.

Anyway, back to the fat shit with his legal drug dealing practice. I just smiled and said all the right things. I listened as Dr. Russ Fitzgerald explained the benefits to a trial of Abilify to keep the thoughts of sharks and repetitive actions away. I listened to the side effects and looked thoughtfully at the glass award on the corner of the desk. It read "Dr. Russ Fitzgerald for Outstanding Professional Leadership. The New York Psychiatric Association."

I thought about picking up that award. I could feel the weight of it in my hand. How I would swing it in a wide arc smashing down onto the fat man's head. I thought about the sound of cracking. The **blood** would fly up and splatter all of the office. How that would be fitting. To slaughter Dr. Russ Fitzgerald and leave his office like the pigsty it was. How gratifying it would be to see that fat hog lying on the ground and grasping at speech. His eyes darting the way a head trauma victim's eyes dart from side to side.

I liked thinking about how wrong the eyes would look, out of sync, out of focus. Then I would cram some of Dr. Russ Fitzgerald's scripts from that prescription pad down his fat gullet. Give the good doctor a taste of his own medicine. HA!

But I did none of that. Instead, I nodded. I said I would think about it and appeared genuinely grateful when the doctor offered me a starter pack of the medication for free. This pleased Dr. Russ Fitzgerald. I scheduled a follow-up appointment for the next month and agreed to start the trial of the medication and call the nurse if the side effects were too troubling for me. I nodded and imagined I would not be troubled in the least by the side-effects.

I was pleased with myself that I was able to wait until leaving the counseling center to find a trash can for the small brown package of pills. I shoved it deep into the trash can outside the student union with disdain. That fucking guy. Like I'm going to take that poison. Three weeks later, I called and left a message to cancel my appointment with Dr. Fitzgerald, explaining I had a difficult test to study for and would reschedule after Thanksgiving break. The counseling center was busy so they never followed up with me again. Easy. Predictable. And fine by me. More than fine, really. I was careful to have no more "outbursts that interrupted the academic learning environment." Dr. Hawkins and Dr. Fitzgerald faded into the background.

Now here I am, sitting at my desk with a wastepaper basket filled with the Sneaky Snatch Snake's word vomit. I have a different problem on my mind today. Something that requires intentional action.

I stand up and reach under my bed to take out the small safe I keep there. I unlock it and take out the leather-bound journal. This is where I write down my best ideas. Chapter 5:3, "The spider's web is created over time and is a result of practice." I'm not like those other idiots tipping their hands for all to see with their legacy tokens and writing about who they will kill on Facebook. Making YouTube videos about their hit lists. I read about those. I've studied. I'm smart enough to know that anything I write down on the computer can be found easily. The sharks, the school, the government; all three working in cahoots. They could track me that way. I know that and I'm aware. But my journal, well, I learned from my run-in with Dr. Robert Hawkins to be smart about my research and planning. To be quiet. Stealthy.

I open the journal and take out my pen to begin a new page. I write one word at the top and then underline it a few times. I write it in all caps. For emphasis.

INITIATION.

I continue writing, flipping backwards and checking my notes.

I'm slightly embarrassed to tell you this next part. It's personal and I think you will judge me. But I've shared so much already and I'm starting to feel like you might be able to understand. Maybe just a little.

Here's the thing. As I'm flipping and checking my notes, I look down at my stiff erection poking pleasingly against my jeans. I grin.

Apparently, I'm excited about what is to come.

Don't be a fuck about it.

# Chapter 3
## New Orleans, Spring, Tuesday, 4:45ᴾᴹ

**W**agner sat on the corner of St. Peter and Royal leaning against a long, iron post supporting the overhead gallery of an apartment.

He wore washed-out jeans and faded boots. A Rolling Stones t-shirt hung off his tall, thin frame. The shirt was faded with age, as was he; both held onto the vibrancy of times past, a floating red balloon against the stone grey of an office building.

She caught him by surprise. Not an uncommon occurrence for Wagner, to be caught by surprise in New Orleans. It was a town prone to shock and wonder, given that its inhabitants were often soaked in gin, quinine, and their unfocused thoughts.

What had she said? Her words plagued him like a song he couldn't stop humming. Something about people waiting. Somewhere. People waiting for him.

A musician across the street strummed a guitar to a small gathered crowd. Wagner listened to this music and closed his eyes; his mind drifted and he thought of marauding pirates, Otis Redding, and silver lockets. It was one of those rare, warm, spring days that lacked the substantial heat common to New Orleans. The heat was coming though; Wagner could feel that unbearable, heavy warmth. The humidity moistened everything it touched, leaving the city and its inhabitants damp throughout the day.

He was across from Rouses Market, a small family-owned grocery in the center of the French Quarter. He sat on the stone curb that separated the sidewalk from the street. A few blocks over was Jackson Square. The square was an open expanse of palm trees, benches, and a large statue of Andrew Jackson riding his horse, Duke, at the battle of New Orleans. The massive cathedral stood with its three prominent spires stretched out above the grass and stone. It was a central place in the city. A place where the city's poor and lost stood shoulder to shoulder with the rich and achieving, to the betterment of both.

He thought again of the blonde girl who whispered in his ear. And "girl" was a misnomer, an artifact that came with being in his early forties. The woman was probably around 19 or 20, though it was hard to say with certainty. The quality and timbre of her voice unnerved him more than her touch. There was something hypnotic about her voice that laced her words. Some kind of magic underneath. After she spoke, Wagner turned to see her more clearly. She breathed a last word to him and faded like an apparition. It was all so familiar to him. She was familiar to him. A memory from another time.

The kid across the street played his battered guitar to the tune of Bob Dylan's classic "Tangled up in Blue". He was in his late twenties or early thirties, kind of on the young side to know Zimmy. He wore those skinny jeans that were popular these days and a vintage looking black t-shirt with a busty 50's pinup straddling a record player. A washed-out green canvas strap hung across the t-shirt's white lettering—Vinyl Vixens. A steady crowd passed as they went about their shopping and sightseeing. They saw the musician briefly, in that absent-minded way a person clicked through the channels on a television when they were unsure of what to settle on. No one noticed him for long.



The song hung in the air as the people passed. A couple in their sixties crossed the street and the woman shook a half-folded tourist map in her hands. She gave off a rushed and frustrated annoyance, clearly wanting to be somewhere else. The man, undoubtedly her long-suffering husband, tried to keep up. He watched the sights around him with a tourist's smile. He reached into his wallet and took out a dollar, ready to drop it in the musician's open guitar case. The wife realized what he was going to do and forgot all about her map. She swatted his hand and ushered him past the guitar player.

"God damn it, Charlie. You don't have to give every bum a quarter to buy a bottle of old grand dad," she gruffed. His hand fell to his side in response to her scolding. It was an old and practiced movement. Wagner took in his expression. Resigned. Defeated. Numb. Charlie had been there before. He'd been there for 40 years.

The musician continued the song without missing a chord. He watched the couple with a distant look. He'd seen them before. The melody swam in Wagner's head. He tried to remember the first time he heard this song. College maybe? He always liked Dylan. He liked "Tangled up in Blue" because it was hard to follow, jumping around in time and space, changing characters and locations all along this underlying thread. It was a likable song, but also a disquieting one. There was this thin, haunting nostalgia; a faint undertone pulling the listener toward some illusive crescendo. The more you tried to follow, the more lost you became.

The song gave Wagner a feeling of déjà vu. Thoughts scurried away before he could put his finger on it. Just like the girl.

Two teenagers came out of the market talking to each other with animated expressions. They shared a bag of Zapps BBQ potato chips. Each took a long pull from his respective bottle of Coca-Cola before moving into the sun. The boys looked to be fourteen or fifteen.

A young woman crossed in front of Wagner. She had a tattoo of a white rabbit on the back of her upper thigh. The rabbit was flying a kite. The tail of the kite was made to resemble thin strips of tangled paper. She had grey-white hair that hung in a swoop over her right eye. She wasn't nearly old enough to have grey hair and the juxtaposition of her hair color and age was sensual. She wore a loose shirt, cut low across her chest. Her skirt was high, showing off her athletic legs. She wore black boots with the handle of a knife reaching out of the top of the left one. A heavy bicycle chain circled her waist like a belt, with a brass lock securing it in place. She walked fast, like she had somewhere to be, but then paused to listen to the music. A faint smile crossed her lips. She walked over to the musician and bent down to place a five-dollar bill into his open guitar case. Wagner looked at the tattoo and her legs for longer than he should have. She was very pretty.

The woman stood and gave the musician a kiss on his cheek and whispered something to him between the verses as he strummed. He missed a chord change, his first mistake since

Wagner had sat down to watch him. Then he thought for a moment. Had he sat down? I mean, of course he had because he was here. But Wagner had trouble recalling that exact moment. What was he doing before he was here on the street corner? He shook his head free of these thoughts and returned to what was in front of him.

The woman continued down the street. She turned once, offering a glance back at the musician over her shoulder. Wagner watched her leave. He imagined she was accustomed to men watching her.

He found the entire exchange highly erotic. Which wasn't unusual in New Orleans. Sex permeated the city, as plentiful as the cracked and uneven sidewalks. A block away, a dozen strip clubs flashed their neon signs down the expanse of Bourbon Street. Women in bikinis and lingerie stood outside the deep-set doorways of the clubs fronted by male barkers calling to passing tourists. The barkers barked, "You look like you could use some whiskey and some tits in your face!" "Come on in! Give it a try. No cover. Cold beer and hot women!" New Orleans wasn't coy; she sold sin and decadence on every cross street like Lucky Dogs from a cart.

Wagner was intrigued by the tattooed woman. She made him curious and pulled him from his fog. He wondered why the rabbit was flying a kite. He thought about what the rabbit meant. If she knew the musician or was just teasing him. What had she whispered that made him miss a chord? It was an occupational hazard for Wagner—curiosity, thinking deeply about things. He thought about the rabbit in *Alice in Wonderland*. He wondered if it was a kind of 'Drink me!' sign. He thought about the rabbit as it looked at its watch and ran, late for the party. That was the feeling; like the rabbit was trying to tell him something.

He took his leather wallet out of from the front pocket of his jeans. It had a small notebook and pen attached to it—a gift from long ago and a favorite possession. He jotted down the woman and her tattoo. There was something there he might use later in a story. A writer's sketch. Now she was further down the street and he could no longer make out her tattoo. Wagner's eyes drifted up to the curve of her thigh and how the short skirt perfectly captured her backside. He contemplated her in a base way and felt slightly guilty for that.

Well, fuck it, he thought. Maybe Bourbon Street tonight. It was good to remain congruent; match his geography with his philosophy. He learned this trick long ago, surfing with the moods and thoughts that swept into his mind. He turned back to the guitar player.

*She was married when we first met, soon to be divorced*
*I helped her out of a jam I guess, but I used a little too much force...*

A disheveled man wearing cutoff jeans and a dirty Saints t-shirt walked by pushing a light blue bike. The bike had a black and red sticker that said, "Pirate Alley Ghost Tours" and had a Jolly Roger skull and crossbones in black and white. The man could have been in his late twenties or early fifties; he had one of those faces.

The man saw Wagner looking at him and he was off to the races. "Hey man," he said. "Wannna buy a bike? Five bucks!" Wagner had been here long enough to give a small smile and gestured 'no thanks' and looked back to the guitar player.

"Come on! It's a good deal. Almost new bike!" he said.

A tall man wearing a fedora stopped on his way into Rouses and overheard the conversation. "Leave him alone. No one wants to buy your stolen bike."

Saints t-shirt looked irritated. "I didn't steal no bike. This here's my bike. I'm selling it."

Fedora laughed and went into the market muttering, "Sure…a brand new bike for five bucks. Deal of a lifetime."

"You don't know nothin'! It's my bike an' I'm sellin' it!" he shouted at Fedora, who was already out of his earshot. He shook his head and continued down the street in search of some new customers for his bike.

This was the music of the city. The man played his guitar.

*So I drifted into New Orleans, where I happened to be employed working for a while on a fishing boat, right outside of Delacroix…*

He was lost in his thoughts and jotted them down in his notebook. Images of a red coral necklace, a worried young woman with a luxury purse and a rain gutter next to the St. Louis Cathedral. This is when she had come up behind him and whispered to him. The intimacy of her closeness surprised him and he turned to look at her.

She was young and pretty; someone Wagner would normally be happy to have invading his personal space. She was thin, small, and her mannerisms made him think of a pixie or a fairy. Light and playful. He absentmindedly closed his notebook and listened.

She wore the colors of the earth, tan and brown, her dirty blonde hair tied into dreadlocks. She watched him with green eyes and an intense curiosity. She tilted her head and smiled at him. A large hound dog gathered itself protectively by her side, tethered with a rope leash. Her worn blue canvas knapsack lay on the ground at her feet. She regarded Wagner with interest.

## Wolf Howling

"What did you say?" he asked.

She smiled again and shook her head slowly. Mischievous. She picked up her bag. Her dog heeled without being called. She gave Wagner a look that was both playful and challenging. Her eyes seemed to tell him, "You already know the answer to that question." There was an enchanting quality to her voice. She offered nothing more and walked away.

Wagner called after her, "Hey! Wait!"

Nothing. The girl walked down the street and was gone.

He wanted to call after her again. He wanted to ask what she meant. Something about people waiting for him. Something about a bar? The musician continued his song. Wagner listened half-heartedly and debated the merits of chasing after her.

*She was working at a topless place, and I stopped in for a beer*
*I just kept looking at the side of her face, in the spotlight so clear...*

He stood slowly, a balanced mix of stretching and overcoming the inertia that held him to the curb. Déjà vu struck and his head swam. This all felt so familiar to him. He walked across the street and took a few dollars out of his pocket and dropped them into the open guitar case. The musician nodded at him and played on to the next verse.

*But me I'm still on the road, heading for another joint*
*we always did feel the same,*
*we just saw it from a different point of view*
*...Tangled up in Blue.*

A bar? That was what she whispered to him. Something about people waiting for him. Wagner had no idea what any of that meant.

No one was waiting for him. He was alone in the city. What did she mean? He took some tentative steps and the guitar player watched him. He tried to remember if he had heard this song played here before. Maybe. Yes, maybe he had. But he couldn't quite remember when, and there was something different about it this time.

The harder he pushed into that memory, the more slippery it became. He wasn't sure about this new mix of feelings. The emotions were uncomfortable and built in his mind rather than abating. The guitar player continued with other songs. An Eagles tune, then Clapton, and a really good rendition of "Ain't No Sunshine" by Bill Withers. All older songs, but he sang them well, with heart. Still, none had the effect on him like "Tangled up in Blue." There was something about that song, in this place, at this time; something that evaded him.

Wagner's déjà vu lingered. Did the guitar player know him? Had he seen him in the Quarter before? Maybe it's just the memory of this song that pulled him back to college. That feeling of nostalgia again. Uncertainty mixed with familiarity; an odd cocktail, like absinthe and chartreuse, competing flavors, but intoxicating nonetheless.

Wagner opened the door to Rouses. The aisles in the store were oddly close to one another. There was barely room for two people to pass side by side. He walked past the two registers at the front and nodded to the security guard. He wasn't sure what kind of crime he was hired to prevent. Maybe shoplifting? Keeping the homeless out? He didn't know. He found what he was looking for past the front alcohol case and down the left to the cold beverage section. He took two long cans of Abita beer and walked back to the cashiers and security guard. He paid for the drinks and went back outside.

The guitar player had moved on and was replaced by a large black woman. She had drawn an even larger crowd as she belted out an

Aretha Franklin-worthy version of "Respect" before dropping into a salacious version of Nina Simone's "I Need Some Sugar in My Bowl". Some tourists had taken over Wagner's favorite spot on the corner. They stood in a group smiling and clapping along with the song. Wagner leaned up against the gallery support and listened to some songs. He thought about buying her CD. He drained the first Abita and made his way through the second and started to find a comfortable buzz.

He needed a distraction. Bourbon would offer that; a neon-bright cacophony of sound and vice. It would dull his mind and help reset things; help him focus. Wasn't that the thing to do when you can't remember a word? When the memory of it just dangles on the tip of your tongue. Like the lure the fish wouldn't quite take. The trick was to let it go, free your mind. Let it hang out there in the periphery of your thought. And when you don't expect it, that's when it would materialize. Wagner thought about cold Abita beer and Jameson on the rocks. He thought about Jackie. He wondered if she was working. Maybe that was how he could figure out what the hell was going on. What the girl was all about.

The black woman had been at it for quite some time and told her crowd she had one more song to share with them before taking a break. She chided them to "share some of your own cash in the tip jar." She picked it up and shook it. Some in the crowd looked sad at the idea of her finishing. Others simply cheered her remarkable voice. Several dozen people were now pushing at each other for a better position to hear. When she began to sing "When the Saints come Marching In", Wagner took this as his cue to start marching out.

Wagner felt this discordant mix of excitement and worry. He had not been feeling much lately. All these emotions were new. Ever since he left Boston and made New Orleans his home, he had been floating, drifting. Until now. Until the girl. He felt antsy, like he should go somewhere. He should do something. But what?

As he walked away from her, he listened as she sang and her voice became lost in the crowd.

*We are traveling in the footsteps, of those who've gone before*
*But we'll all be reunited, on a new and sunlit shore...*

# Chapter 4
## New Orleans, Spring, Tuesday, 4:45ᴾᴹ

Ella crossed St. Louis and Royal and walked with determination down the street. She was pissed. It wasn't the first time Kara had left her high and dry on the rent and she was pretty goddamn certain it wouldn't be the last. And then someone stole her fucking bike. She was madder at herself for this than the thief. So stupid that she didn't use the chain. Just a quick cup of coffee, she thought. Such an idiot. Just what she needed. Just to make an already-shitty day all the more shitty. Or was that shittier? Whatever.

She shared a small apartment off South Dupree on the outer limit of the Quarter with Kara the Vapid. The apartment was relatively cheap and close to where she worked, which were the only positive adjectives one could use to describe the place. The two had been roommates for about six months. Kara was physically striking, tall and athletic, and carried herself with a confidence that was addictive—certainly Ella's type. What Ella first took for some layer of class and elegance with Kara faded when she experienced the whirlwind of a mess that trailed behind her in the apartment. That and her always forgetting to pay the fucking rent. That was the god-damn kicker.

Royal was stacked with tourists wandering and gawking. Ella had a love/hate relationship with them. Sure, they paid her bills and kept her off the street, but shit, they were annoying. She worked at the infamously famous Pirate's Alley Ghost Tours, located in the heart of the Quarter. It was a one stop shop/bar/ tour company designed to separate as much money from the tourists' pockets as possible. Pirate's Alley reminded her of Mrs. Lovett's shop in Sweeney Todd. The bodies go into the pies; everything worked in a symbiotic relationship toward a singular purpose—to rob the general populace of their money. Eh, it paid the bills. Barely, but still.

Ella led ghost tours on Monday, Tuesday, Thursday, and Friday nights. The other nights, she bartended at Peg-Leg Pete's, the bar Pirate's Alley was centered around. She poured absinthe and explained nightly to ignorant, know-it-all hipsters why she didn't set said absinthe on fire like they did at the Absinthe House on Bourbon. "This is the Parisian preparation," she told them. "The Czechs light it on fire; we don't do that here." That was the party line. The real reason was that another bartender, Hope, had almost set the entire place on fire by knocking over a customer's glass because she was high as fuck during her shift. That story, however, lacked the historical flavor and pizazz that Peg-Leg Pete's wanted to convey.

Ella brightened immediately when she saw Coop rocking out "Tangled up in Blue" on the corner near Rouses. The lyrics jumped all around, from strip joints to basement apartments. The melody was catchy and she listened. While the song never did make much sense to her, the musician playing it certainly did.

She caught a sideways glance from an older guy sitting on the curb listening to the guitar player. He was cute, and she saw him checking her out. She gave him a faint smile. It's funny how guys don't realize that women know when they are looking at them. Not that it is always a bad thing, certainly not from the guy in the Stones t-shirt and boots. Ella thought he was cute.

Across the street, an old man sat with his back against the wall outside of Rouses. He had a dark blue backpack with lettering and odd symbols scrawled all over it. Crazy person behavior. He had two cardboard signs next to him and a black and red baseball hat with a few coins cradled inside. The city was always asking for something.

She took out a five and made eye contact with Cooper and leaned over in front of him, knowing exactly where his eyes would go. She could also feel Mr. Rolling Stones looking at her from behind, which wasn't an entirely unwelcomed or unpleasant feeling.

She stood, leaned in, and gave the guitar player a sisterly peck on the cheek while he strummed between the verses. Then she whispered in his ear, "When I leave, watch me. Because later tonight, I'm going to fuck you silly."

Cooper missed his chord change and gaped at her slack-jawed as she began walking away. Once she was a few yards down the street, she glanced back, glad to see he was watching her, and not overly surprised to see Mr. Rolling Stones doing the same. On any other day, she would have stayed and teased both of them some more. But not today. Today she was going to visit Kara at work and get the fucking rent.

Ella quickened her pace down Royal and turned toward Bourbon and The Bayou. Her happiness at seeing Coop faded quickly and was replaced by her anger about the rent. And even more, she was pissed at Kara for making her have to chase her down. She had told her last night that she needed the money and it was already three days late. That was the part that irritated her. She might be late to her job in order to fix this problem. Like she didn't already have enough shit to deal with.

A young woman walking a dog passed her. She was pretty, small, and thin, and there was something about her that caught Ella's eye. She wasn't her type, but she was cute. Something mysterious about her. Eh, you spend enough time sleeping in doorways and you grow an air of mystique about yourself. Ella picked up her pace and let her thoughts drift away from the woman.

She crossed Royal and passed Lost and Found, an antique shop she liked to visit when she was wandering. She had made friends with the proprietor, who was well traveled and would exchange stories of Europe and history. Everything there was way out of Ella's price range, but that never stopped Ms. Golightly from having her Danish and coffee at Tiffany's, so why should it stop Ella from dreaming?

Ella walked onto Bourbon Street; Amelia was out front of the club. This changed Ella's mood some. She had always liked Amelia and she particularly liked her when she was wearing that black bikini with some bright pink heels. Fuck, she had nice tits. She nodded at Frank, currently playing the barker side of his barker/bouncer job description. He was built like a tank and busting at the seams of his suit. He had short cut, cropped hair and looked like he was ex-military. He smiled at Ella and said, "Cold Beer! Hot Women! Come on in!" Ella laughed deeply and a bit too loudly and gave Amelia a hug.

"Hey Mel, they got you working the street tonight?" she said.

"I know, right? Like a common whore," Amelia said sarcastically.

Amelia reached up and tousled Ella's smoky grey hair. "I love this color and cut, by the way. New?" She ran her hand over the smooth part of Ella's head. "So smooth, love it, love it." She bounced up and down some as she repeated how she loved Ella's hair. Ella watched her breasts struggle against the fabric of the bikini and bounce with her. She tried to think of her stage name. She thought maybe it was some kind of small forest animal? It slipped her mind.

"Just last week. Figured I was due for something new. I've already been getting some better tips on the tours. Guess the paying customers like a tour guide who has a little strange going on," Ella answered.

"Well, I'm a fan," Amelia said and looked out at the crowd again. A trio of likely frat boys from LSU in their purple and gold were passing by. Amelia ignored them and looked instead to some thirty-something conference attendees wandering down Bourbon with the wide-eyed reverence of small children on Christmas morning. She put her hands on her hips and pushed her chest out. She made a pouty face at them as they passed by her station outside the club and beckoned with one 'come hither' finger.

Ella directed her gaze to Frank and away from Mel's posing and pouting. "Kara's working, right? I need to talk to her for a few minutes." Frank said she was and gestured Ella to the door. Ella nodded a 'thank you' to Frank and entered. It was cold in the club, the A/C blasting on full. It was also sparse, with some regulars spread out in the dark, but nowhere as busy as the place gets on weekends when the tourists are out in full swing.

Ella immediately saw Kara. She was hard to miss. She wore a low cut, black dress that gave her an air of sophistication. She was talking to a balding man in a worn orange polo shirt and jeans. Ella thought about a tiger circling a gazelle; a predator circling its prey. That poor bastard was about to be separated from a substantial sum of money. In the hopes that this would be the case—maybe some of that money could be used to pay the rent Kara owed—Ella pulled up a bar stool and waited. She figured it would be bad juju to mess with Kara and a client.

The bartender came up leisurely and smiled. "Hey, love the hair, Ella."

Ella smiled at Jake and found herself staring at his smooth chest underneath his black t-shirt. "Well, hey yourself stranger. How's business?"

"You know, I can't complain. Been a little down lately in the drink department, but I think she's doing okay." Jake gestured over to Kara and her client. She had begun to run her hand across his shoulder and trailed it down his arm. Jake set a shot of whiskey down in front of Ella and waved her away when she reached for her purse. Jake said, "On the house, professional courtesy. So, what brings you in today? Lap dance with Mel?" He smiled his charming smile.

"No, not today." Ella met his gaze. "Actually, need to have a heart to heart with Kara about the rent again. Shit's getting old."

Jake nodded. "I get that. I had this roommate after college that was a nightmare to get money out of. He was fine with getting me the rent on time, but trying to get money for phone, cable and utilities was like pulling teeth." Jake thought a moment and then took out a fresh shot glass and poured himself a shot along with a second for Ella.

He raised the glass, "To cheapskate roommates, may karma bite them in the ass."

Ella tapped her shot glass on the bar and then raised it and said, "I'll drink to that. Cheers."

Across the club, Orange Polo had spilled a drink on his shirt, no doubt while being distracted by Kara's cleavage. Kara didn't miss a beat and took a napkin off the nearest table and began brushing him on his shirt and pants. The stage name Kara used was Ella's suggestion: Cassandra. Snakes and prophecy. All of the negative connotations of the name flew over Kara's head. Ella thought it was a good use of her master's degree in Folklore and Mythology.

Kara/Cassandra led her mark to the back of the club. The manager took some money from Orange Polo and Kara led him into the back rooms and the VIP lounge. Ella wondered what went on back there. She imagined a lot of frustrated groping and touching. New Orleans was known for its lax policy between dancers and patrons.

Jake pulled her from her thoughts by asking, "How's work treating you these days?" He ran his shot glass underneath the bar sink, giving it a detailed wash.

Ella looked thoughtful. "Not too bad. I like the tour stuff more than the bartending, no offense."

Jake nodded. "None taken—I get that. Waiting bar can be a feast or famine. Either bored as hell or struggling to keep up. I get it."

"It's just easier with the tours. You can get a little lost in the script. Makes the night go faster," Ella said.

A few young men came into the club hooting it up, dressed in casual clothes and wearing beads around their necks. The ringleader, a tall dark-haired man, wore a "Party in NOLA" shirt and had the largest collection of beads. On stage, a petite brunette with short cropped hair came out dressed in silver bottoms and matching top. She wore high heels and drew the attention of the newcomers quickly. Ella watched as she danced, and Jake began some more detailed bar prep for the evening. He sliced up a few dozen lemons, limes, and cucumbers for various cocktails. The majority of the patrons at The Bayou ordered beers, but some would order the occasional fancier drink, and he liked to be ready for that.

Kara led Orange Polo out of the VIP rooms; his shirt and jeans looking somewhat disheveled. Ella was impressed that Kara still looked like her same elegant self. She supposed it was that same look that made Ella enter into a lease with her. Likely that look had gotten her pretty far in her life. Ella had trouble imagining many people telling her "no" to anything. Kara excused herself from her client and walked over to the bar. She smiled brightly at Ella, like she didn't have a care in the world. Ella thought that was likely an accurate view from Kara's perspective. Ella did not share this view.

"Ella!" She gave her a squeeze of a hug. "It's good to see you. Did you come to keep me company on this dreary and slow shift?" Kara asked.

Ella was gruff, "Something like that; can we talk?"

"Sure. What's up?" Kara asked.

"I don't want to be a bitch about this, but the rent was due three days ago and I don't have your share."

Kara put on her best smile. "Oh, was it rent day already? I completely missed it." She asked Jake for a cigarette and he obliged her by sliding one over from the pack he kept by the bar.

Ella had heard this before. She wasn't amused. No "sorry" or "here's the money." It's as if she needed Ella to ask directly. Like some kind of fucked-up power play. Ella tapped her fingers on the bar impatiently. "Yes, three days ago. Rent's due by the 5<sup>th</sup> of each month. We've had this talk."

Kara ignored her and asked Jake for a light. Jake took a silver Zippo out of his pocket and flicked the lighter to life. He was very dexterous. He brought the flame close to Kara's cigarette. She puffed once, twice, three times a lady. Jake made the Zippo disappear into his pants. Kara regarded Ella, "It's really not a problem. I'm not sure why you get so worked up over it."

Ella rolled her eyes. "Listen its $400. Do you have it?"

Kara regarded her with slight disdain at the mention of the amount of money. Like it was some kind of social faux pas to bring up the actual amount. "Of course." She withdrew some bills out of the clutch purse that was hanging off her wrist. She counted out two hundred-dollar bills and ten twenties. "Here." She pushed the money over to Ella across the bar like she didn't want to have to bother with the mundane aspects of life. Like it was below her station. Ella was pretty sure she had not had all this money until a few minutes earlier.

"Thanks!" Ella said brightly and tapped the money into a neat pile and put it in her back pocket. Getting into an argument with Kara was like punching a bowl full of Jell-O. It never ended well and was unsatisfying. She learned to avoid protracted engagements with her.

Well, mostly.

Ella had to admit to that brief period where she had fucked Kara. There was no getting around that. It started late one night when Ella was very much on one of her back and forth rebounds with

Cooper. God damn musicians. But that was another story. They ended up in Kara's bedroom, which served as a metaphor for their short-lived relationship. Kara's bedroom and Kara's rules. It was always about Ella seeking Kara out. Not that it would have led to anything significant, but it was one of the things that had helped end it almost as soon as it started. Ella had always been fiercely independent. Living with her parents in Amsterdam during her formative years had seen to that. The fling with Kara, and that really was a better word for it, fling, was fun, short-lived, and ultimately ill advised. Ella left Kara at the bar in much the same way she left her in the bedroom. Quickly and very much aware that she had escaped a more prolonged encounter that could have ended badly.

She thanked Jake for the drink. He said back, "Anytime, beautiful." She checked the time with him. She should be at work. Her shift would be starting soon. Ella stepped out of The Bayou into the dusk of Bourbon Street with $400 in her pocket.

Mission accomplished, now to get to work.

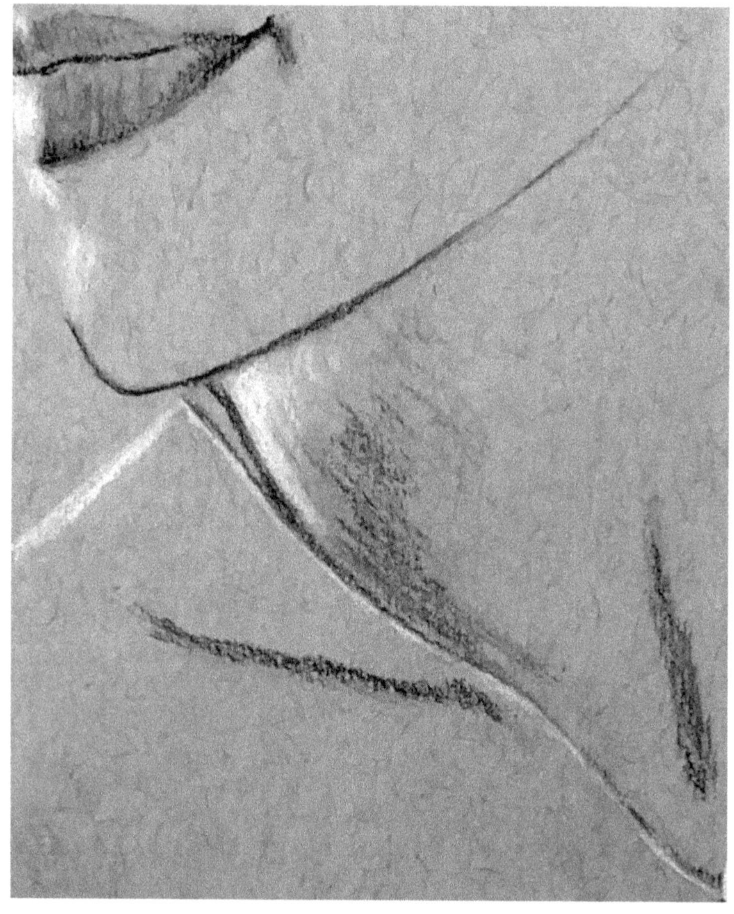

# Nightfall

# Chapter 5
## New Orleans, Spring, Tuesday, 6:30ᵖᵐ

She walked through the city after her meeting with Sinclair. He hadn't followed her, which was not surprising. She had been followed, stalked, attacked, heckled, yelled at, and cursed; but not by Sinclair. His reaction was always the same, a kind of befuddled confusion. Like someone waking up from a deep sleep.

Oliver padded along behind as they passed a striking woman with white hair and a tattoo of a rabbit flying a kite. She looked rushed. She had seen her before and she wondered if she was part of Sinclair's story. She was certainly his type, she thought, as she looked at the knife sticking out of her boot and the bike chain slung around her waist. Ripped right from central casting.

She stopped at the Café Au Lait for a coffee. The establishment had a large green and white awning that protruded into the street and offered the most wonderful air conditioning. Oliver liked the place because they had a water bowl set up outside the café and they welcomed dogs. She tied him outside and then ordered her coffee. She liked the bitter taste of the chicory they added to the iced coffee. She sat down at the table and pet Oliver in that spot behind his ear that he loved so much to be scratched. He stretched up to feel her touch and then settled back down into the coolness of the evening surrounding him.

She thought about Sinclair. Maybe this time would be different.

Maybe this time would be the last.

# Chapter 6
## New Orleans, Spring, Tuesday, 6:30ᴾᴹ

'm a writer too; just wanted to let you know. Maybe not like the pale Galilean or Mr. Sinclair, but I've been working on something. Something big.

I'd see it as a how-to guide. Maybe a bit of a roadmap for those who want to follow in my footsteps. I know I'll be famous; it isn't a question of that. So few people who become famous realize they will be famous beforehand. That's the difference for me. I know. I've prepared. I've studied their mistakes and will use them. Just like the Hopi tribe used all the parts of the buffalo. Chapter 1, verse 7, by the way.

I put away the journal. It's done anyway. *The Book of Albert.* I'm sure you'll read about it someday. You'll be able to quote chapter and verse. But for now, as they say, it's time to put away the childish things and become a man. Was that Lou or God? One of the two. Either way, it'll be quite a show. You're probably thinking that I'm going to kill that BITCH. That would be a reasonable assumption on your part. And I won't lie to you and tell you I haven't thought what it would be like to cut her. To feel my knife in her.

It's a Microtech Halo Tanto blade, in case you want to know. $579. Pricey. There are cheaper knives, of course. But this one I like the most. It's an automatic that fires when you hit the ambidextrous thumb switch. It opens with an audible thwank that I find very satisfying.

I first saw it on TV. Jack Bauer used it on *24*. And oh, man. I knew I needed to have that knife. Just that one. It was perfect. I didn't need any other knife. This was the one for the job. I saved up; I'm smart. Counted my pennies and quarters working that bullshit lifeguarding job at the community pool. Saved up and ordered it online. Everything is available online, nowadays.

You probably think, even at this early stage of us getting to know each other, that lifeguarding was a bit of an ironic job for me. Fair enough. But it was an easy job that gave me time to think. There was something in staring out over the water in a glazed way watching people doing their thing. The old fuckers showing up at 5:55am in their swim caps and goggles to swim back and forth doing laps at the YMCA pool. The best part was they didn't hassle me about reading while I watched the pool. I went through a good number of books while watching the fat and lazy frolic in the water with their little piece of shit kids. Sartre, Nietzsche, Mill, Camus. I like to read philosophers; gain some insight into the different ways that people live their lives.

Anyway, back to stabbing that fucking BITCH. Oh, I've thought about standing over her. Sure, you can even say I fantasized about it. The technical phrase Dr. Robert Hawkins would use is "fantasy rehearsal." Not that he would ever say that directly to me. But like

I said, everything is available online nowadays. And I'm a good student. I figured out that term.

So, let's go with that, shall we? Let's fantasize and rehearse. Here I am; standing above her while she sleeps. My hand covers her mouth and she wakes up. I watch her struggle against me. I press the button and its eyes widen as the knife comes erect in front of it. I slide the blade into it, past her saggy right tit and in between the ribs. I am inside it and the blade enters its heart. There is that moment where its eyes grow bigger still. And then they flutter. And then they go vacant.

Oh, man. Just this thought gets me hard again. No time for that, though. It's time to pack. I have a big night ahead of me. Chapter 2:12, "The desire of your heart can be hard like the rocks of the greatest mountain or soft like the lush meadows." I'm going lush meadows.

The pack on the bed is a military style bag made by a company called Maxpedition. You can Google it. Go ahead. I'll wait. I can't do everything for you. Don't be a fuck about it.

Anway, it's the black one. A little longer than a standard college student backpack. I need the extra length to get the FNP90 rifle in there. That baby was another favorite I saved up for. Like swimming laps. Back and forth. Watching those dollars grow.

The rifle is short, first of all. About the length of a toolbox. The barrel is snub-nosed after I shaved it short. It originally came with a longer 12-inch barrel, but that almost doubled the length of the weapon. Too big. So, I read up on the Internet and shaved it down to two inches. Ha! First time anyone would be happy to go from twelve inches of hard steel to two! See, I can be funny. I have a pretty decent sense of humor.

I first saw this rifle on the TV show *Stargate*. It was the standard weapon that all the soldiers carried. I researched it some. And man, was it cool. The best part is the 50-round clip that slaps into place on the back end of the rifle. There are ways to make it automatic, but that is a rookie mistake. Chapter 4:1-2, "I shall be the hammer in your hand, the bullet in your brain. Choose carefully the weapon, the method of destruction." I have woven my web carefully.

Oh, have you figured it out yet? I think you're starting too. I think you are very much starting to figure out what is going to happen. But it's important that you know this: I've studied. I've studied how to do things better. It won't be like what you've seen on TV. Paddock did pretty well in Las Vegas. He tried to steal some of my thunder. But he didn't have his *Book of Albert*. Chapter 2:22–23, "This is not a question of chance, but rather of focus. This is not a fact, but it is a truth." Maybe if he spent less time playing thousand-dollar hands of video poker and fucking around with casino lawsuits and more time being focused and dedicated. But that's the big problem, right? No one spends any time being intentional anymore. They just expect the world to fall at their feet and start sucking. Well, that isn't how it works. You have to prime the pump before the world sucks your dick. Make a plan, my man. Chapter 1, verse 1.

I've practiced with it in the swamp outside of the city. I got pretty good at firing three-round bursts on a target and then acquiring a new target. So, it is a pretty easy task to go through a group of twelve or fifteen people with three-round bursts before having to reload.

My tactical vest with two Kevlar plates is in the bottom of the bag. The front has an extra three magazines for the P90 across the center of the chest. There are three smaller magazines that ride lower on the belt. These are for the Glock. A small sheath made from black plastic holds the knife. Chapter 4:7–8, "The pale Galilean, the prophet carpenter, had many hands and many tools. Be prepared when your hammer slips and fails you."

The Glock 9mm was my first gun. That's where some people get lost in this. Going overly fancy or complicated with the weapons. I have two, with 200 rounds for the FNP90 and another 68 rounds for the Glock. Four 17-round clips. Well, technically 69 rounds because I always keep one in the chamber of the 9mm. Ha. 69! See, that's the stuff. Get the world on its knees.

The pack holds the two weapons, the knife and the tactical vest. It's a little heavy, but that's okay by me. The weight is reassuring, really. I like the heft of it. I've been working out at the university gym more over the last two months. Getting in my core and cardio.

I put the journal back in the safe with my copy of Sinclair's book. That's where the police will find it if I get caught. When they come across *The Book of Albert*. If this was the only copy, well, then I think they might try to keep it from going public. That was the problem Harris and Klebold ran into at Columbine. They didn't have the vision. They didn't know they were going to be famous. Not really. So, they didn't plan well. Chapter 1, verse 2, boys. They didn't think about their exit strategy. How they would get their message out.

Did you know that? I'm not sure if you did. I've spent so much time on this research, I have to remember that other people don't know the things that I know. The two kids at Columbine recorded about four hours of VHS tape encouraging people to follow in their footsteps. But the police found it and the FBI blocked it from being released. Fucking asshats. Not that it would have made a difference. I'm sure it was just the two of them rambling on about anarchy and how people had bullied them.

Anyway, I made a copy of the book and will mail that out when I am ready. Send that right to the local newspaper. Let them get a good gander at it. Not to some fucking worthless TV station where some fake-tit, blonde-haired bitch would read my words. Or some gay, Ken-doll, coiffed faggot. They would just fuck it all up and then Mr. Conrad and Valentine would have their way. That's not the way I want my message sent. I'm looking for that old-school journalism.

The Korean kid at Virginia Tech got it closer. Mailed his package out half-way through his attack. Made sure his message got to the people. The problem, of course, was that his message was a bunch of lunatic, whiny bullshit. Not me. Nope. I have other plans. Give the people something top shelf. Something high quality. Inspire all those kids out there who need someone to believe in. I'll be their Christ. My words will be the rock on which they build my church. Chapter 8:4, "Be nourished as you read my words and follow my path, my way."

I take the Pirate Alley Ghost Tours brochure and slip it into the pocket of my black jeans. I'm wearing a pair of well-worn boots and my favorite shirt, dark grey with a fox outline on the center of it. It says above the fox, "I don't give a…" Get it? Fox. I don't give a fox. Ha! I found the shirt one afternoon while I was wandering the French Quarter. A small shop off Chartres. It was an instant buy for me. I told you, I have a sense of humor.

Actually, it was the thing that started up the first conversation between the BITCH and me in the cafeteria. She had asked to read my shirt. So, naturally, that's where I had complimented her on her hair. Tit-for-tat. Like saying lines in a play. We started having lunch together and found a lot of things in common between us. She worked at this tour place in the Quarter. But this isn't really about her. I don't want you to get that impression. If anything, she was just the latest in a series of disappointments. My anger has abated from this morning about her ending things.

Chapter 2:14, "When the heart is hardened and the grievance is fierce, focus is lost." But of course, verse fifteen is what it is all about, isn't it? My path became clear. Crystal clear.

Like that asshat who crashed his plane said, "my bags are packed and I'm ready to go." The other stuff I need is in the car already.

Huck is down the hall, probably fucking around with some other guys. Did I tell you I have a roommate? I do. His name is Huck. He's from Alabama. Tall like a fucking cornstalk and with about the same level of smarts. But if I make it out of this alive, then I need him for the cover story. Simple as that. Huck also has the best illegal fireworks. I know this because I bought a pack of 4 M-80s off him last week.

Huck is two rooms down with Dan and Keith. Like I knew he would be. I knock quick and open the door without waiting for a response. And here they are. Dan and Keith playing Madden on the PlayStation. All of them sucking down beers. They jump up when I come in.

"God damn it, Al!" Keith says. "We thought you were Niles. Fuck." Huck and Dan take their beers out from the makeshift hiding place between their legs.

Niles is the RA and has already threatened to report Dan and Keith twice this semester for drinking in their room. He hasn't done it so far but is fond of talking about his three strikes and you are out policy.

"Nah," I say.

I sit down on one of the open chairs and watch these grown men push buttons to make little computer versions of men throw things and catch things and run, on the enormous TV. Another example of how society is slowly coming apart at the fucking seams.

I wait for the right moment and then share that the BITCH had told me to go pound sand.

"Wait. Pause this," Huck says and Dan hits pause. "What happened?" Huck asks, genuinely concerned.

"Yeah, guess it wasn't meant to be," I reply, putting on my best sad face for the audience. I tell them the story, leaving out the ripped-up note and other thoughts I have already shared with you. They wouldn't understand.

"Fuck, man. You can do way better than her, anyway," Huck says and Dan and Keith nod in agreement. Well, Dan nods, Keith looks longingly back at the TV and seems to be willing the pause button to be pushed again to resume play.

"You know what, Al? We should all go get fucked up tonight. All four of us should go down to Bourbon and tie one on. Smack some tits and get wasted." With this, Dan nods more vigorously and says, "hell yes," and Keith puts down the remote and seems on board as well.

Well, I think to myself, this is going better than I had thought. I continue with my plan.

"Turns out, my parents sent me some money this month…" I take out a wad of $20s, about 600 bucks that I have been saving up since the beginning of the semester. "Maybe this will get us started."

"Fuck that," Dan says. "I'm buying for this one. We'll get you some nice pussy."

Dan's parents are well off and Dan has a history of spending his money on the group. Partly why they have a 70-inch flat-screen TV and PS4 in their room. This is a second unexpected bit of good news. I certainly could use the money for other schemes in the future.

"That's the rule man. Get you a fucking lap dance and get you over that shit," Huck says.

"I can drive, if you guys want. Give me a half-hour and finish up the game. I'll text and meet you outside?" They agree and I go to get ready.

My car is parked outside in one of the larger lots on campus. I have been putting together everything I need in the trunk for the better part of the semester. Ever since I read Sinclair's book, I knew what my life was leading to. And I knew what it would take to pull it off. Another critical error people made was planning these attacks when they were pissed. They got sloppy. And when the target was known to them; someone they hated, they wanted to die and didn't care as much about the bigger picture. Which again, is a trait my generation is known for. Lazy and sloppy, disengaged and aimless. Chapter 2:17–18, "For many, the crusade becomes about the artfulness of it. If those who will perish are not known to you, then your strategy will reflect this."

But not me. I have been planning and thinking about all the different arcs a plan could take. Like fireworks, you can control the chaos in the gunpowder and explosions if you just plan it out enough. Have some goddamn forethought and patience.

The car is a Chevy Impala. A couple of years old. Silver. Nothing fancy, but reliable. That is important. I don't need to take any chances on the thing breaking down or getting stopped in something speedy or fancy looking. I put the backpack in with some shopping bags and other supplies for the night's fun.

They meet me outside and we drive from the garden district to downtown. Huck wears a green-wave t-shirt and Dan has on this shirt that has an upside down hanging opossum on it. On the bottom of it are the words "Marsupial loving." This makes absolutely no sense to me, but that's okay, because neither does Dan. I still laugh at it because I have this thing for novelty t-shirts. I don't give a fox. Keith wears shorts and a white shirt. He makes some comment about the dancing being better if there is less fabric between you and the pussy. Ah, Keith, my exotic dancer connoisseur.

It's a quick ten-minute drive over to the public parking lot on Decatur. That's where I leave the car. This is a good thing, because Keith is also wearing enough cologne to supply a New Jersey nightclub. "You have to smell nice for the ladies," he says. I roll my eyes. The four of us pile out of the car and head down Iberville toward Bourbon.

Huck slaps me on the back and says, "Oh man! We are gonna have some fun tonight!"

I smile and pat my hand down twice on his shoulder in a show of roommate comradery.

"This is just what I needed!" I say to Huck. And he smiles that dumb redneck smile right back at me. Dan and Keith high-five each other and we walk into the night.

Just what I needed.

*I am the lightning before the thunder.*

# Chapter 7
## NEW ORLEANS, SPRING, TUESDAY, 6:30[PM]

agner walked the stretch of St. Peter between Royal and Bourbon; a block of unfiltered, straight, no-chaser New Orleans. There was a Voodoo shop and two bars on the left of the street, and on the right, there was Pat O'Brien's. Preservation Hall was at the end of the block pumping out historic jazz twice a night to throngs of aficionados cramped in a non-air-conditioned wooden box of a room. That was the end of St. Peter.

Then Bourbon Street was upon him, a cacophony of sights, smells, and sounds. The street offered two faces to the world, like a tide that pulled out and drew in. Each morning, as dawn made its abrupt arrival in the city, the pavement of Bourbon was scrubbed and cleaned by a legion of city employees. Their vast machines sprayed water and collected trash and discarded beads, clearing every imaginable fluid that could come out of a person. The cleaning was a baptism of sorts; it washed away the decadence of the night before, or at least, washed away the outward manifestation of the self-indulgence and excess.

Bourbon's other face was neon-bright in the darkness. The florescent buzz was harsh and brilliant against the hazy, charged night. Smoke rose from the street as it wound in a stretch of hedonistic, drug-addled expanse that would have given Hunter S. Thompson a run for his money. *Fear and Loathing in Las Vegas*, Southern style. Bat country, indeed.

Bars named Crawfish Daddies, Tropical Escape, and the Drunken Alligator repeated each block down the street. The ubiquitous Lucky Dog vendors offered their tasty meat treats from hotdog-shaped carts. Artists and performers competed for attention at each cross street and hoped to make some money off the hundreds of tourists who wandered slack-jawed down the thoroughfare. Cigar smoke hung in the air and neon green plastic drink containers littered the street. Throngs of partygoers filled the balconies, tossing beads onto unsuspecting passersby.

These days, more men than women raise their shirts to the crowds throwing beads from the balconies and galleries above. They gesture wildly with hopes of being rewarded with plastic trinkets, whistles, and catcalls. The few women who lift their shirts do so after bargaining for higher end feather boas and second-tier tossable offerings. The plain and basic beads struggle to keep up with inflation. The times, oh, they are a-changin'.

As Wagner stepped onto it, Bourbon was far from the quiet of a slow Sunday morning, but equally distant from the shoulder-to-shoulder pandemonium of Mardi Gras. Most of the deadly sins were still on parade. Sloth, gluttony, lust, greed, wrath, pride, envy…all dancing second line-style through the streets. Wagner crossed onto Bourbon from St. Peter, where the Oyster House met the Paradise Lost bar. To the left, Canal Street waited with its streetcars, large hotels, and casino. Between St. Peter and Canal was the heart of Bourbon. To the right, the street crawled slowly to something of an end, much like the party, transitioning from the initial excitement and intoxication to the slow crawl of drunkenness and incapacitation. An assemblage of shady characters and low bars attracted those looking to double down on their evening debauchery. Like Virgil leading Dante, the street progressively descended into increasingly intoxicating and delightful wickedness.

As darkness fell, Bourbon was in transition. Parents pushed strollers filled with wide-eyed children down the sidewalk. Exotic dancers emerged from darkened strip clubs offering enticements for those on the street, bikini-clad siren songs to the wandering hoards. Cars were blocked off from the street by large metal barriers. Horse-mounted police had begun their nightly patrols.

The clamor of Bourbon distracted Wagner from the girl who had whispered secrets to him and the musician who played the Bob Dylan song. An entertainer dressed in purple and gold in the style of a medieval court jester bounced and joked his trade to a family of tourists. He lured them with juggling and witty banter. A drunken partygoer took a picture of his girlfriend next to the police horse. She spoke in a high-pitched, excited southern voice and told the mounted officer all about her horses back home. The beleaguered officer looked at her with disinterest and listened to her story while he surveyed the street.

A tall, thin, black man stood frozen and immobile in his white tuxedo and a top hat decorated with the good old USA stars and stripes. He stretched out in the middle of the street with one foot resting its heel very far from the other. In one hand, he held a leash attached to a stuffed toy black dog that sat on the pavement next to a bucket for tips. He didn't move until people drew near to the stuffed dog. Then he would jerk the leash with a small, practiced movement that made the dog jump. People laughed and left crumpled dollars in their wake.

A group of young, and presumably homeless, early twenty-somethings sat around a box containing a large black dog lying on its back. A poorly drawn cardboard sign explained their dog had died and they needed money for a proper funeral. It wasn't clear if the dog was dead or merely playing dead. Wagner walked by the macabre scene a bit faster.

Several tarot readers sat at fold-out card tables on the corner of the next block. Their tables were scattered with skulls of various animals, brightly colored candles, scarves, shiny trinkets, and faux gems. Multiple decks of cards lay amidst the tables. They sold a taste of the future based on present hints and tells. Not a bad way to make a living. Everyone wanted to believe in some higher power.

Wagner ducked into Paradise Lost. This was a favorite stop for Wagner since he moved to the city. He knew most of the bartenders and many of the regulars. He wondered if the girl who talked to him earlier would be here. Maybe this was where he was supposed to meet whoever was waiting for him. He looked around but didn't see the girl or her dog. Instead, he saw Jackie behind the bar. This made him smile.

She wore a black tank top with thin shoulder straps that showed off a good amount of skin. The straps of the tank top and those of her bra competed for space on her shoulder. Wagner liked to watch as her tattoo weaved in and out of his view.

Jackie was his favorite for a number of reasons. He was happy to see her and was caught off guard a bit at how much he missed her. "Hey Jackie, how's it been?"

She returned his smile brightly and hugged him across the bar, "Hey yourself there, Wags. Whatcha up to today?" Her dirty blonde hair was tied back in a loose ponytail and her mermaid tattoo swimming through a deep blue sea drew his eye, as usual.

"Just wandering the city. Taking it easy. Busy?" Wagner ordered a double Jameson rocks and beer chaser from her.

"Not too bad today. Tourists in and out. Wish it would pick up some, make the shift go faster," she said, pouring his whiskey.

An assemblage of older regulars lined the barstools. There was a fair amount of gawking at Jackie's more than generous curves that were displayed nicely in her tank top. Nina Simone played from the jukebox, announcing she was feeling good. It was a nice respite from "Don't Stop Believin'" and "Blurred Lines," the pervasive songs that drifted from the majority of bars in the Quarter. Another reason Wagner liked it at Paradise Lost.

The bar was dark and matched the nightfall outside. Jackie put the Jameson down along with his beer. "Writing any?" she asked.

"It's been a little dry lately. I probably need to go find a war to fight in or something, like Hemingway. Get all inspired and such," Wagner replied.

"Well, drinking helped him too, right? So, you're on the right path. Just don't follow that road all the way to the end, you know?" She winked and smiled at him. Hemingway committed suicide by putting a shotgun to his head and pulling the trigger with his toe.

Wagner had a thing with Jackie a couple months ago. They started seeing each other and he had walked her to his place after her late shifts. The sex was good and he liked her company. She was smart and clever. His eyes drifted down and he thought about lying in bed with her. Maybe the sex was even better than good.

He began to ask her how she had been. He thought about starting that old conversation about why things hadn't continued with them, but was interrupted by a pair of middle-aged women wearing beads and Mardi Gras hats in purple, green, and gold stepping up to the bar. Jackie touched Wagner's hand across the bar, as if she read his thoughts. He forgot how she could do that with him. Anticipate what he was thinking. She walked to the end of the bar by the door and asked, "What'll it be ladies?" The conversation went back and forth until they both settled on a hurricane, that sweet, red punch-flavored rum drink favored by out-of-towners.

The whiskey burned as it went down Wagner's throat, a pleasant warm sensation that he followed up with a deep swig of Abita amber. Tom, an old-timer at the bar, slapped Wagner on the back and gave him a Willy Loman salesman smile, albeit lacking some teeth.

Tom wore a well-loved white seersucker suit and Oxford shoes. The suit was discolored from years on the street. His shoes were scuffed and worn.

"How you been, Wags?" Tom asked as bits of nacho fell from his mouth. He wiped the pieces away and then brushed his hands clean on his suit with some mild embarrassment. "Sorry 'bout that. Grabbing a little snack here." He gestured to the remainder of nachos piled high on a white coffee filter in front of him on the bar.

"I'm doing well, Tom. Can I get you a shot?" Wagner caught Jackie's eye without waiting for Tom to respond. Tom never refused a shot; waiting for a response wasn't required.

"Thank you, kindly," Tom said, his hand tipping an imaginary hat.

Jackie finished making the beaded tourists their hurricanes as they happily chatted her up about restaurant recommendations in the Quarter. Jackie offered some suggestions in that bright and encouraging way she had with people. She had a great personality for a bartender. She talked to people with respect and interest. Making new friends was something she liked to do. She also knew the bartender's secret; regulars tipped better. She cultivated new customers where she could.

Wagner set a twenty and a ten down on the stained bar and took a go-cup from the stack on the bar next to the small containers of cherries, lemons, and limes. The go-cup was a staple of the city. Liquor laws were lax in New Orleans and people were allowed to walk around with open containers as long as said alcoholic beverages were in plastic cups. No glass permitted. He poured the beer into a large cup with a single palm tree on a small island surrounded by a blue ocean. He thought of that ocean and her mermaid dancing in the waves.

He wanted to talk to Jackie about what had just happened with the girl, maybe about what had happened with them, but he wasn't sure she would understand either conversation. Maybe that was why things didn't work with them. She got some of him, more than most, but that wasn't quite enough. And in some ways, it was worse than not getting him at all.

"I'm gonna wander for a bit; we need to catch up. Want to get some food after you get off?" Wagner said.

"I'd like that—come back later and get me. I'm off at 11." Jackie gave him a squeeze on the arm before he left. He thought about them in bed together at his apartment. Had it been two months ago? He remembered Faulkner curled up on her lap while he made her breakfast. She had this way of sitting on the bed with her legs crossed and her hair down around her head, watching him. He missed her.

He stepped out onto Bourbon as dusk faded, the darkness of evening moving in impatiently. Zydeco music played from a NOLA souvenir shop across from Paradise Lost. Racks of t-shirts with fleur de lis and "Saints Who Dat?" printed on the front lined the walls of the establishment. Shelves held the orange canisters of Café Du Monde coffee and boxes of beignet mix.

Masks and beads hung from the display stands in the traditional colors of purple, green, and gold. They represented justice, faith, and power, though that subtlety was lost on most, particularly those wearing beads with little penises attached. The religious traditions of the city had long been co-opted by perpetual spring break college students, mid-life crisis fifty-year-olds trying to recover a lost youth, and the alcoholics pouring in from one day to another. When it came to Mardi Gras, the reason for the season fell a distant second to making a buck.

Wagner walked down Bourbon and headed to The Bayou, about two blocks down from St. Peter on Bourbon. A neon green sign hung over the street like Spanish moss hanging from a cypress in the Louisiana swamp. An imposing, well-dressed bouncer with a fleur de lis neck tattoo stood outside the club. He wore a dark suit and held a stack of "no-cover" cards in his hand. A short redhead stood next to him wearing a black bikini and pink fuck-me heels. The stretched fabric of the bikini struggled to cover her body. Her freckled white cleavage drew the attention of people on the street walking by the club.

The redhead in the black bikini reached out and touched Wagner's arm and tried to guide him into the club. He offered little resistance. Wagner finished his beer and tossed the cup into the bin outside the club. The bouncer slipped a no-cover card into Wagner's hand and walked behind him through the dark entryway. He was the easiest sales pitch of the day. He thought of Jackie stroking Faulkner on his bed. Maybe when he picked her up later they would rekindle things.

The club was neon-new and the air-conditioning kept the temperature around permafrost. Electronic dance music filled the air. The seats were half full, with a mixture of frat boy types, business men, and party-goers; the last group identifiable by the piles of beads on their chests and green plastic hand grenade drink cups in front of them on the tables. The club had a single stage. Its current occupant was a long-legged blonde. She climbed her way to the top of the pole, inverted, and started a slow seductive spin to the stage floor.

Wagner sat at the bar and watched her descent and enjoyed the approaching easy soft fog of a perfect buzz. Not drunk, not sober, but that no-man's-land of peaceful, easygoing feelings. The stress and oddness of his encounter with the girl had faded. His distraction seemed to be working.

A hand came out of the darkness and pulled Wagner close. He had that startled feeling of déjà vu again. The woman attached to the hand dragged Wagner's attention away from the blonde spinning on stage. The sight of her broke his mind. She was tall. Easily six feet in her long stiletto heels. She wore a black cocktail dress, cut low and deep. The dress clung to her body like a second skin. A black and gold onyx charm hung in her décolletage, which drew Wagner's eye. It had this obsidian quality that pulled him in like a black hole. She was stunning and elegant. She had Middle Eastern features and a sophisticated grace. Perhaps Egyptian? She talked to him in a low, salacious voice while she ran her fingers slowly up and down his arm. She never lost eye contact with him.

"You know what you need?" she purred.

Intrigued, Wagner answered, "I don't. What do I need?"

"Well," she said and shifted her hand from his arm to his shoulder, "I think what you need is a drink. To start with, at least."

"I'm not one to argue with a beautiful woman. A drink is just what I need. How about you? What can I get you?" he asked.

"Gimlet," she said.

"Classy," Wagner replied, and she smiled at him and their eyes locked together. Time slowed and he saw something ancient in her. Something primal.

Reluctantly, Wagner broke eye contact with her. He closed his eyes, feeling muddled and murky, like she had hit him with a blackjack sap. He lowered his head and turned to where he imagined the bartender was standing. This helped clear his mind. That slow, deliberate motion was done with molasses speed. Though he still felt her grey eyes watching him in the darkness.

Wagner opened his eyes again and focused on the bartender finishing with another customer at the other end of the bar. The bartender walked over at Wagner's gesture. He wore a tight, black t-shirt with a deep-v and nodded at Wagner when he ordered her drink. He reminded him of a *Twilight* version of the vampire.

"How about you?" the bartender asked as the knife sliced the lime cleanly in two. He rimmed the inside of a martini glass with half of the lime. "What'll it be?"

"Negroni? Light on the vermouth?" Wagner figured he'd stay in the gin wheelhouse with his new companion. The Dylan song and the girl with the dog were far from his mind.

"Well gin? Bombay? Tanqueray?" he asked for Wagner's preference.

"Hendricks," Wagner said, and the bartender reached from behind the bar for the short, dark bottle of Hendricks gin.

Mr. Deep-V mixed her gin and lime together and then turned to pour the Campari and gin into Wagner's glass with a splash of sweet vermouth. He put a lime twist on her martini and set it in front of her. "Here you are, Cas." She smiled and thanked him.

The bartender added an orange twist to Wagner's drink and set it down. Wagner paid and turned his attention back to the woman in black.

"I'm Wags. It's nice to meet you," he said over the electronic music pounding around them from the stage. Over on the main stage, the blonde crossed on all fours, catlike.

"Cassandra. Pleased to meet you as well," she said.

Cassandra sipped her drink and looked at him with her grey eyes without saying a word. Wagner couldn't take his eyes away from her lips. He rocked his drink around in his hand and thought about what to say. He remembered the old adage about not talking first when negotiating a deal. This, in turn, made Wagner think about making a deal with the devil. An odd thought.

Cassandra's skin sparkled with a faint dusting of glitter in the light of the club. She caught his gaze on her lips. Wagner looked up and smiled, discovered staring.

"So, what brings you to my city?" she asked. "Business or pleasure?"

He liked the way she said pleasure. Her hand moved from his shoulder to the back of his neck. Her nails raked softly against his skin. He thought again about vampires and deep-v black t-shirts.

"Always a little of both. I'm working on a book," Wagner answered.

"Ah, a writer type. I like writer types. What's it about?"

"A story of intrigue and deception. The great American novel."

"When you want something, all the universe conspires in helping you to achieve it," she said and sipped her drink.

Wagner was surprised by her quote. "Coelho, one of my favorites. You do like writers." *The Alchemist* was indeed a favorite of his. The story of a boy who followed his dream. Not a common reference for her to have made. An odd thought again.

"Well, I like to stay well-read," she said. Those eyes again. There was something so familiar in them. She had a deep, soft voice and long black hair that came down across her breast. Wagner's gaze was lost in her cleavage, drawn to the silver locket that hung against her perfumed skin. The scent was familiar; some flower he couldn't quite place. And there was something about her necklace that seemed off.

"You know what you need?" she asked, and Wagner felt her fingernails cross the back of his neck.

He sipped his drink. Tried to play coy. "Another drink?" He was not good at playing coy.

She smiled at him. Bewitching. He would build pyramids for her if she asked.

He glanced at her cherry red lips again as she took another slow sip of her drink. For the briefest of moments, the tip of her tongue was against the red lipstick. There was something reptilian about the way she drank.

"You already have a drink." She brought her hand down from his neck to his thigh. "Such thirst doesn't always permit for tact. You need to take me in the back," she told him this with a definitive certainty.

Wagner smiled at the line. She was intriguing.

"To the back?" He raised an eyebrow.

He knew what she meant, but also enjoyed the tango here, the seduction of it. The VIP section of the club. Lap Dance. He had already made up his mind about going back with her. Something to further help clear his head from the day's twists and turns. A quick dance, another drink, and then he would head back to feed Faulkner and try to write again. Then he would get Jackie for dinner.

Her eyes shone and the purr returned to her voice. "Well, here's what I'm thinking. It's darker back there. More private. Maybe give us a chance to talk more about your literary aspirations."

"Ah, so you would encourage me? A muse, of sorts?" Wagner answered back, playfully.

She liked that word. Her eyes brightened. "Yes! I shall be your muse. Come to the back with me and I will certainly inspire." She stood with her drink in one hand and took Wagner's hand with the other.

On stage, the music faded and the blonde collected her scattered outfit. She gathered the dollar bills strewn across the stage, sweeping them up like leaves on a November sidewalk. The bills went into a velvet purple Crown Royal bag looped around her wrist. She shimmied into a red dress and disappeared into the darkness behind the stage.

Cassandra led him back into a room separated from the hallway by a red curtain. There was a dark leather couch in the corner. She guided him to it. Wagner sat and watched her adjust the single, dim light emanating from the corner lamp with a beaded Victorian style shade. There was a mirror behind the couch and Cassandra looked at herself, her hand slowly following the lines of her hip and upper thigh. She guided Wagner over to the center of the couch. A low table was in front of them. She moved like a snake through high grass. Without effort.

The music shifted to a new club mix. She stood above him and drew his attention to her breasts. One hand slid across Wagner's chest and the other behind his neck. She pulled him closer. Jasmine, he thought. That was it. She smelled of jasmine. Cassandra moved in time with the music, her legs against his. Wagner put his hand on her hip. The bass pulsed in time with her against his body. Her mouth was close to his ear and this reminded him of the girl again. Her hand moved quickly from his neck to his throat, she was assertive and pressed him back against the wall. Wagner was surprised by the boldness of her dominance. His head fell back and he gave her the control. Her tongue licked at his ear. Was it a purr or a hiss? He couldn't tell.

The first song dwindled and transitioned to a new melody, not an easy thing to differentiate, given the overpowering techno beat overlapping the songs. Cassandra straddled Wagner and he thought about a line from the television show *Mad Men*, "Every woman is a

Jackie Kennedy or a Marilyn Monroe." Cassandra was a Marilyn; everything she did was a breathy seduction. It was impossible to imagine her doing anything without it being wrapped in honey and lace.

"Another dance?" she asked.

"How about a few more?" Wagner responded.

The alcohol swirled his thoughts and the girl and her dog were once again far from his mind.

Cassandra's eyes were warm and she smiled slyly. The tip of her tongue licked the corner of her lips.

The music from the main stage pounded into their space. Cassandra began to move with the music, sliding slowly out of her dress. Wagner followed the black charm hanging between her breasts like a rube following a carny's pitch. His breath caught when he looked at that charm. Something about it. Déjà vu again. This faded when she rested her hands on his shoulders and brought her breasts close to him again. Their softness against his face and the smell of the exotic flower hung around him. Cassandra slid over to the side of the couch and brought her long leg up across Wagner's throat. She pushed him against the back of the couch and looked at herself again in the mirror. She was strong and held him there. Wagner's hand drifted across her hip and waist in the low light of the room.

"So…do you trust me?" she asked.

"Sure. I trust you," he said.

"That probably isn't a good idea." She regarded him mischievously.

She raised Wagner's shirt, the union jack and iconic Rolling Stones lips scrunched together around his neck. She brought her hands across his chest and ran her fingernails on him, holding the rudraksha seed he wore around his neck on a black string. She bit him gently on his neck. Then a second time, harder.

The pain hit Wagner like an electric shock. He had been bitten before this way. He thought back to the bedroom that overlooked the Quarter with Jackie, but she had never bitten him this hard. His control further slipped away, his grip lessened as the alcohol anesthetized his thoughts. He wasn't sure what Cassandra would do next. It was rare for him to be out of the driver seat. He felt lost with her, though he didn't seem to care much.

Cassandra pulled him into a kiss. Her tongue swam with his.

It was the kiss that drove Wagner from the club. The taste of gin on her lips. Something too familiar about that. Like he had kissed her before. Goosebumps rose on his arms and then he felt like he was falling. Vertigo. Something was wrong. Like a fly that realized a spider was near. There was a deep, resonate, hollow sound in the darkness pinballing against the machinery far below. A gear had slipped.

The thoughts returned. The girl and her whisper. There was a floodgate that had opened; water rushed through the sluice, threatening to drown him. Was there someplace he was supposed to be? The more he thought about this, the harder it became to stay in the club. He felt late. White Rabbit late. Very late.

He pulled back away from Cassandra's kiss before the full panic hit him. He edged her back away from him. She was surprised by this. Those haunting, purring, hissing seductive eyes were gone. She looked like an actress who had forgotten her lines. Wagner figured very few of her clients left her mid lap dance. Not a woman like her.

He mumbled something about being sorry and pressed a hundred-dollar bill and some twenties from the clip he kept in his pocket into her hand before he made his way back to the main club. A petite girl with short-cropped brown hair was now on stage. Wagner settled his tab with the deep-v bartender and made his way to the door with a sense of growing panic.

He stumbled out into the darkness and onto Bourbon Street. He looked down at his arm and saw the sparkle of glitter. Glitter in the dark.

He walked faster into the cacophony of lights and sounds.

# Chapter 8
## New Orleans, Spring, Tuesday, 6:30ᵖᵐ

ith $400 in her pocket, Ella walked down St. Peter's Street toward Pirate Alley Ghost Tours. Her shift started at 7pm, and she had to get into costume before her first tour of the night started. She had two tours tonight, at 7:30pm and 9:30pm. They usually lasted about an hour or so, depending on how much she liked the group. She hoped to finish up with enough time to get to get to see Coop open for Vinyl Vixens tonight at 11. He had been trying to get a gig lined up for a few weeks with his band, and she wanted to offer some support.

She turned the corner and the entrance to the bar was in front of her. Like many of the old buildings in the city, it had a blend of old brick, painted shutters, and iron work. A large, gaudy sign, somewhat out of place among the historic nature of the city, hung above the arched doorway with a ghost being chased by a pirate.

The bar itself was a combination gift shop, gathering place for the tours, and old-style pub. It had an open seating arrangement, with a dozen or so tables, each set with four of five chairs around it. The bar was made from old, worn cypress and had aged brass fixtures and foot rests. The stools had leather padded tops studded with brass tacks to hold them in place. Most were filled with the first night tour starting shortly. Night ghost tours were always more popular.

There was a podium where the restaurant hostess would typically stand as you came in the room. It was made to look like a series of poorly placed crates and had some frayed rope hanging off the sides. In a touch of brilliance, someone had glued several gold and silver colored doubloons to the floor next to the check in. Instead of a restaurant hostess, there was Liv. She was short, with long black hair and dressed in a flowy red skirt, white blouse, black bodice, and more than ample cleavage. She smiled briefly at Ella, but her thoughts were clearly elsewhere and she seemed distressed.

Ella paused. Usually Liv was more upbeat, part of the reason she beat out Hope for check-in duties. "You doing okay, hon?" She rested a hand on Liv's arm. Liv pulled her arm back in pain. "Sorry, clumsy. I hit it on a shelf at the library." Ella apologized and worried after her some. She seemed truly shaken up. Liv continued, "I'm not doing great, to be honest." She had an uncharacteristic quake to her voice. "But look, you have a full crowd and have to get ready. I'll fill you in a little later."

"Hmm, boy trouble? You know I could help, come over to my side for a visit." Ella offered a flirtatious smile, trying to make Liv laugh. It didn't work. Liv was holding back tears now and seemed panicked. A family of four waited behind Ella to check in for their tour. Ella took the hint.

"Okay, tell me later. Promise?" Ella asked. Liv perked up some, "Promise."

Ella rested her hand on Liv's back and gave her a squeeze. They weren't close friends, but she always liked her and always greeted her when her shift started. Liv was in college, working to pay the bills in between classes, studying, friends, and having a life. Ella made a mental note to check in on her after her first tour group. She walked past the check-in station and into the main room.

It was about half-full, with five or six guys at the bar and another dozen families, older couples, and a group of women with "Brittney's Bachelorette Bash Bitch!" t-shirts sitting around the back tables. Two small children were having a mock sword fight with the plastic swords they had taken from a barrel with a sign that read "cutlasses for sale: $9.99." Other shelves held buckets filled with eye patches, plastic hook hands, cast-iron looking rubber handcuffs, "real metal" doubloons, plush ghost dolls, and Ghost Alley Pirate Tour stickers with the Jolly Roger in red and black. Ella had seen it busier, but this was a good-sized crowd for the night. She wondered who was taking out the first tour. Maybe Dave.

Hope was behind the bar wearing a laced corset and leather pants. She had a light blue tricorn hat on with a matching choker with a silver metal coin bearing the symbol of the skull and crossbones. She juggled drink orders from the bar and the waitress working the tables. "Hey Ella," she bubbled at her.

"Hey yourself, Hope," Ella said back. Hope was cute, though not the brightest light on the Christmas tree. But, she was sweet. She had relocated from southern California to New Orleans and had very much kept her San Diego charm, along with some great access to weed, which Hope used liberally. Blonde and thin, her positivity and exuberance surpassed her small frame. She was very popular with the customers, several of whom who were currently pushed up to the bar with drinks and snacks, likely waiting for their tour to start. The bar served some pirate themed food like Parrot Wings, which were regular chicken wings, Dead Men's Fingers, which were little smokies sausages, and something called Captain Malick's BBQ, which looked like pulled pork with a dark red sauce.

Hope set down a double whiskey in a plastic go-cup with two ice cubes. Ella thought, "Alright Hope!" and reached through the throngs of tourists at the bar and took the whiskey with a wink and a "Thanks, babe!"

Hope gave her best "for sure!" The door at the far side of the bar had the sign "Captain's Quarters" above it. The door opened, and the owner came out.

"Avast yea! Scallywags!" Cliff said, waving to his employees and the customers around the bar.

He was an enormous man, often mistaken for being of Samoan descent. He wore a red and black long pirate coat with a black, tricorn cap. He had a wig of long black curls that came down around his head, and well-worn, black leather boots with an authentic looking sword at his side.

"Hope! Ella! Shiver me timbers! It is good to see ye!" Cliff said.

The pirate talk could grate after a while, but with Cliff, it was easier to put up with since he genuinely loved it so much. He was like the ghost of Christmas present when it came to pirates. Just super enthusiastic in a contagious way that made you play along.

Hope responded with, "Aye, Capt'n. No black spotted, bilge rats around today trying to hornswoggle us!" Ever since she almost burned down the bar, Hope was the most enthusiastic responding to Cliff in pirate voice.

Ella waved hello to him and then opened the Crew Only door. It was decorated with an isolated desert island with a single palm tree.

Dave was in the back of the staff room sitting at the computer. He was already dressed in full tour pirate garb: white flowy shirt, brown coat with brass buttons, and leather gauntlets. A dark brown sash hung across his black pants. No real swords were allowed in this establishment. Dave made up for it with a blue stuffed parrot named Zazu, which while technically not a parrot and from Disney's *The Lion King*, was popular with the little kids on his tours.

"Avast ye, ya scurvy dog," Ella greeted as she sat down and sipped her whiskey with her boots now kicked up on the table with the computer.

"Ahoy, wench," Dave came back, smiling to himself, without looking up. "Full crowd for you later tonight. About half a group for the early gig." He clicked back and forth on the computer screen.

"Not too bad, I guess. Maybe I'll get some tips." Ella finished her whiskey, stood up, and walked over to her locker. There was a pirate-themed privacy screen that folded out in a tri-fold, behind which the lady pirate tour guides could change.

"You always get tips. You have tits," Dave said, switching the scheduling software over to solitaire. "Are you planning some kind of Amsterdam-style, anti-fascist coup with that chain and knife?" he asked, gesturing to the bike chain around her waist and the knife handle sticking out of her boot.

"It's not just tits, I give the people entertainment, fucker!" Ella said the last with a flourish and opened her locker. It was nice of Cliff to give them lockers so they didn't have to walk through the streets in their costume. Not that anyone would have noticed. She took off her top. She hung it in the locker and took out her white, low-cut pirate blouse, red boned corset, and black flowy pirate wench skirt.

"Hey, I use what I got, ya know?" she called at him over the screen, "Can you believe this? Some fuck stole my bike!"

"No way. Didn't you have it locked up?" Dave said, moving a King of Spades onto his first column.

Ella rolled her eyes from behind the privacy screen with pirate ships fighting a cannon battle across the sea. "Listen here, rapscallion…sure, that would have been a good idea."

She was pissed at herself for leaving the bike unattended when she ran into PJ's Coffee for a double espresso on the way to get the rent from Kara. The guy making it was super high and it took literally forever to get her drink. And when she came out, the bike was gone. The chain and lock, however, were still secured to her waist.

She unlocked them with a key fastened to her wrist and hung lock, chain, and key on the hook in the locker. She put the $400 from Kara on the shelf under the lock and chain. She pulled her skirt on and added the red sash with silver coins attached to it. It looked a little more gypsy than pirate, but the powers-that-be gave her some wiggle room on accuracy and cultural appropriation.

For the last touch, she took her silver knife from her boot and attached it to the garter sheath that she'd made especially for her outfit. Her father taught her to never travel without a knife. She adjusted the sheath to her thigh and let the skirt fall down around it.

Dave finished his game and watched the cards bounce around the screen pleasantly. It was five minutes to seven and he stood up to go meet his tour. Ella shut her locker and came over to the desk. She laced and tightened the white rope ties that fell over her cleavage.

"Little help?" Ella asked. She turned around for Dave to fasten the corset. It wasn't a traditional laced corset, but rather one that had a series of clasps. Ella had gotten the first few and needed him to finish the top couple for her.

"Sure." Dave latched the remaining clasps and his parrot jiggled all jolly-like as he gave her a final pat on the back.

Ella took up her post on the computer and clicked back over to the scheduling software. Dave gave her a wave and she said, "All hands hoy. Get ye some booty out there."

Dave gave a final, "Aye, Bucko," and left the staff quarters for the bar to gather up his group.

Ella sat and gathered her thoughts while waiting for Dave to take his group and clear out the main room. Liv would check her group in and then she could go out and lead the tour. She had been doing this for a few months and had the tour shtick down cold. Lots of walking and three ghost stories: The Two Sisters, Captain Malick, and Marauding Jack.

She found herself thinking again of varying apartment options, with a growing discomfort of living with Kara and, oddly, back to that man who sat on the street outside of Rouses wearing that Rolling Stones t-shirt. Older, but still kinda hot. There was something about him that stood out in her mind, but she couldn't quite put her finger on it. Like this feeling of déjà vu.

Almost there, but then gone. She looked at the clock. Shit, time to get to work.

Ella stood and adjusted her ensemble, making sure her cleavage was in that sweet spot of eye-catching but not indecent. She grabbed her jade-colored antique bottle from the bookcase next to the desk. Dave had his parrot, Ella had tits and beer. A good night could bring in at least $100 in tips. That and usually a few phone numbers that ended up in a jar at the end of the desk. Dave liked to crank call them on his breaks.

She opened the door and was greeted by a raucous smash as a shot glass shattered against the brick wall near her head. Ella didn't jump. She expected it.

Three girls wearing colorful beads and waving cash lined the bar in front of Hope. They all wore "Brittney's Bachelorette Bash Bitch" t-shirts. A tall, wobbly blonde, who could only have been Brittney herself (her t-shirt declared this), took another shot and threw the glass against the wall. She was all smiles and woo-hoos, along with bright flushed cheeks from the large amount of alcohol she'd consumed during her bash. Ella could only hope that the big day was not tomorrow for Brittney.

Hope said in a chipper, sing-song voice, "Avast ye wenches! I be pouring another cannonball for the next lass! Unless she be too lily-livered to walk the plank!" The three women were, in fact, not too lily-livered and handed Hope another twenty for three more shots.

The shots were served in ice glasses made in special molds. According to the stories, there was a bar on Bourbon Street called The Swamp that used to serve them with some kind of peppermint or spearmint mix. Once they did the shot, the customers would throw the glass against the head of a concrete alligator in the corner of the bar.

Here at Peg-Leg Pete's, the shots were a mixture of fireball liquor and cherry juice that the bar cherries came in. Always efficient in getting people racing on sugar and booze. The trouble was freezing enough of the shot glasses each night. Hope went through several dozen. That was why the Swamp stopped serving them; well, that and the likely lawsuits from drunken tourists on Bourbon throwing rock-hard ice glasses at each other.

Several families jostled for position on the other end of the bar near the front entrance around a raised dais that read, "The Crow's Nest." A stylized, faded and burned pirate map gave them a full relief version of the city with the tour stops marked out. You could see Captain Malick's ship docked off-shore and the spots where Marauding Jack found his victims. The map had lights and its own theme music that was sufficiently creepy to have parents asking if this tour would be "too scary" for their little ones.

Ella called her group to order up front and began her spiel. "Ahoy, me hearties! Are ye ready to hear some of our ghost stories? Not all pirates end up on fiddler's green."

The group paid their bar tabs and purchased some drinks to take on the road. Ella did a group count. There were twenty tonight for her first tour. She walked over to Hope and set her pirate bottle on the bar. She went over to Liv's station and picked up a pile of ghost shaped fans with the skull and crossbones painted in a dripping blood color in the center. Ghost Alley Pirate Tours was written on the top in large letters. The bottom had a scrawl font that read "Dead Men Tell No Tales."

Ella looked over at Liv. She still looked sad, but there wasn't anything to be done about that right now. Ella handed the fans out to her group and went back over to Hope.

Hope took Ella's bottle and set it up at the Abita tap and filled it for her. Hope then winked and said, "This be thirsty work, telling the tales of the dead…" Ella nodded and took her bottle filled with frothy, cold beer. She led her group out of Peg-Leg Pete's and took a deep pull at the bottle as she walked through the door. Storytellers had a long history of drinking; it was to be expected and added to the ambiance.

The pavement outside was uneven. Well, it really was uneven all over the Quarter. Ella stood in the street, playing a bit of a game of chicken with the occasional passing mule-pulled carriage tour, while her group gathered on the sidewalk in front of her. A few of the children played with their ghost signs. Two had cutlasses and were hitting their long-suffering father. Six or seven of Brittney's Bitches leaned against the wall and waited for the world to stop spinning. Two college-aged guys leered at Ella's outfit and made what she could only assume were jokes about plundering her 'booty.'

Ella wiped the beer from her lips and began the first story. She spoke softly and lost the pirate speech. That worked well in Peg-Leg Pete's, but not out here in the dark. Pirates aren't really all that scary, and it worked against the nighttime New Orleans mystique. Her group drew in closer to listen. Even the children let their sabers fall to their side for a moment. The college-aged guys focused more on her words and less on leering at her.

Ella started, "Back in the day, there were two sisters, Madeline and Cora. They lived here." She gestured to a tall, foreboding building with a high, wrought iron balcony several stories above them.

Ella took a moment and surveyed the crowd. Part of good story telling was taking confident pauses. Ella had told this story enough to know it by heart and was able to draw out parts to lure her tour group in. Her folklore study degree from UNO gave her an edge on most of the other guides at Ghost Alley. Not many tour guides had master's degrees in folklore studies.

She continued, "Cora, well…you see, Cora was the older sister. As with most older sisters…" Ella paused again to survey the crowd. She found a family with a young boy and older sister. She made eye contact with the older sister, who was wearing a pink Mardi Gras mask t-shirt. "As with most older sisters, she sometimes was jealous of the affections offered to her younger sibling by caregivers, friends, and neighbors." Ella released her gaze as the girl looked down, her face red. She continued, "Bitter over the fawning attentions and the sweet offerings of affection given so freely to the young.

"Well, Cora was the older sister and she was envious of her younger sister, Madeline. You see, Madeline drew all the consideration from young male suitors. Not that she looked for it. Oh no, not her. Madeline only cared for books and drawing. But this made Cora even more bitter and incensed. Cora raged that Madeline had everything and she didn't even want it. It was the ultimate insult to Cora that Madeline seemed to toss aside things that Cora would have…" Ella paused again and made the last few words strike home, "…well…would have killed for.

"There was one particular suitor who lavished his affections on Madeline. He was an attractive young man by the name of Curtis Locke. He was entranced by Madeline's beauty and even found her lack of interest in him a bit of an intoxicating challenge." Ella gave a brief glance to Brittany's Bitches at this word and continued, "Mr. Locke was a wealthy merchant trader and had made several calls to seek Madeline's hand in marriage. Madeline began to be receptive to his attention and started to talk more to her sister about her growing affections for Mr. Locke." Ella gave another pause and took a swig from her bottle of Abita.

"One night, after witnessing a particularly affectionate, and therefore particularly upsetting, visit between Madeline and the young Mr. Locke, Cora fought with her sister in an argument that turned vicious. In a moment of final, blinding rage, Cora pushed her sister as she stood near the balcony railing. Madeline lost her footing and fell into the darkness. This is where she died." Ella took a slow sip of beer and looked about the crowd. The story had landed well, though Madeline had not. Even Brittney's Bitches were quiet and looking at her intensely. They waited on her next words. Just how Ella liked it.

"Cora was charged for her crime and punished severely by the judicial courts. She spent the rest of her days in prison for her murderous crime. As for Mr. Locke? He was quite heartbroken. He journeyed far away from his home port of New Orleans. He lost himself in his business and thought only of merchant ships and account books to push his one true love out of his mind. Locke never married, nor did he ever return to New Orleans." Ella left this hanging in the air for a moment.

She looked above the crowd and down the street. She walked backwards for a slow few steps and forced the group to follow her in order to hear the end of the story, "To this day, while walking the streets of the Quarter, Madeline's ghost can be seen. She wears a white dress and a wedding veil. Through her cries and tears, she can be heard calling to Mr. Locke.

*"…my dear love, Mr. Locke. My dear, dear love…"*

The group talked about the story as Ella walked ahead and led them to the corner of Ursuline and Chartres. They followed dutifully as she pointed out interesting facts about the architecture and shared stories of the infamous LaLaurie Mansion. Ella led them to an old section of fence on the corner of Barracks and Chartres. There were dozens of padlocks attached to the wrought iron. Ella paused the group and said, "These are offerings people leave for Madeline and her dear love, Mr. Locke. You can come back and leave one if you wish. It's best to keep the ghosts happy in our city."

She walked the group deeper into the Quarter and the adjacent neighborhood, the Faubourg Marigny. She picked a corner that had a flickering gas lamp to tell the second tale.

Ella began, "Captain Malick would prey on the shipping industry. Not quite a pirate, you would find no Jolly Roger on his ship's mast. But he was a thief and would take from those he would come across. He would take from them what was valuable in the cargo hold. And have you heard what else he would take?" She paused, letting the question hang in the night air.

The college boys were at it again. Ella walked closer to one of them and stared into his eyes. He had blonde tousled hair under an LSU cap. He liked the attention from her and smiled at her like he was at a frat party. She eyed the college boy and continued, "Well, that's when things got interesting.

"If you were a merchant ship carrying valuables and you came across Captain Malick and his crew, you were rightly terrified. Losing the cargo was the least on the mind of the ship's crew and captain. Because Malick didn't just want grain and blankets and fine furs and rifles. He wanted something from each ship. Something more..." Ella paused for effect and then continued, "something more personal. You see, Malick was known to be a bit of a sadist, both in terms of his sexual appetites and his baser desires." One of Brittney's crowd chimed in, "sounds like my ex!" and the rest of them started to laugh and pat her on the back.

Ella stepped closer to the group of women and said in a deadpan voice, "They say that he acquired the taste for human flesh when he served for the British navy and was shipwrecked off the coast of Madagascar. The stories are not complete, of course, because most of the crew was lost in the shipwreck. But for those few who lived, well, most of them lost their minds and never spoke again."

Ella paused and moved back into the street. The darkness had settled more here. The noise of Bourbon and the heart of the Quarter had faded. A few of the children had taken to holding onto their parents' hands and scooted closer to them for protection.

"Malick was one of the few that came back to civilization, but he wasn't quite right. He wasn't like those who had lost their minds. It was as if Malick had learned to adapt." Ella waited and looked over the crowd before asking, "You know that old saying about what happens if you stare into the abyss long enough, right? Nietzsche said the abyss stares right back into you." Ella surveyed the dark windows of the buildings above.

Almost absent-mindedly, she continued in a concerned whisper, "The thing is, no matter how much loot or cargo Malick took from a ship, he always took one more thing from the crew. See, the cargo he took was for his crew of not-quite pirates. The bounty was split and profits were made at the next port. Malick divided the winnings up and paid the sailors a fair wage. He bought them drinks and got them laid. He kept them happy. He kept them content.

"But the thing Malick wanted wasn't money. It wasn't happiness and it wasn't contentment. What he wanted was to watch others in pain. What he wanted was that taste of flesh from the underside of the arm of his captives. That fresh, wet flesh." Several people in the group made "oh, gross!" comments at the description. Ella liked that reaction. She had worked this story more than the other ones. She liked this performance.

She continued, "He had a knife, Malick did. They said it was taken from the savages that had molested and killed most of that British crew. It was said to be a cursed blade, sharp and steady in Malick's hand. They said he would cut away just a bite at a time. Sometimes, he would put it right into his mouth and sometimes he would use the little urn in his quarters filled with white hot charcoal. There was a small metal grate at the top of the charcoal, where he would lay the flesh he had cut away with his silver knife. He would sear it on the one side, all the while looking into the eyes of the person he had chained to the wall of his cabin.

"So, while Malick took the cargo and treasure from the ships he boarded, he would leave the crew unharmed. This is why so many have heard the stories of Captain Malick. He left many survivors behind to share their stories." Ella paused, as if ending the story. This was her favorite part.

"Well, I should say this. He left most of the crew unharmed." She stood close to LSU Hat and looked him in the eyes. He looked back, a bit unsure and definitely without his flirtatious smile. "There was always one he would take. The ships he ravaged were mostly cargo ships, though sometimes passenger vessels. In either case, he would gather the passengers and crew together, much like you are gathered here. Then he would draw his knife and start to pace."

Ella smiled, reassuringly, "I can see some of you starting to worry. The little children are scared and their parents concerned. Perhaps you thought this would be a gentle voyage into the night. Perhaps now you are realizing you've bitten off a bit more than you care to chew." She nodded and offered warm gestures to put them at ease. She continued, "Well, these stories are just stories. You have nothing to fear. Rest assured, Captain Malick is long dead and sleeping with Davy Jones. Way down in the salty deep."

The group relaxed some and smiled. They seemed to brush off Ella's warnings and show her what brave little tourists they were. Ella smiled back at them.

And then she let her smile drop, "Although…" The group's tension returned. "They do say his spirit is restless. It was not content to be confined to the deep. That it can only find peace when it inhabits someone in his city. But only when the night is just right, in the city he called home. The Crescent City."

Ella raised her skirt to the side as the group watched her intently. She drew the knife from its sheath on her outer thigh. The silver caught the light just so, and it shimmered in the darkness. She looked thoughtful as she paced back and forth in front of her tour group.

"He liked the different flavors, Captain Malick did. I think that was the truth of it, but not everyone knew that part of the story. He liked the way different people tasted, the way a wine connoisseur likes various vintages and varietals." She played with the tip of the knife as parents held their children close.

She walked and spoke to them, "Sometimes, he would choose a young girl. I think he would choose her because the flesh tasted pure; clean and crisp like a chardonnay. He said it would just dissolve on the palette. You wouldn't even have to chew." Children in the group sunk back away from Ella.

She walked and spoke, "Other times, it would be an older man. Here the meat was more seasoned and matured. It tasted of life. Like a bold red wine. There was no telling how Malick's proclivities ran and what his desires would be."

Ella paused in front of the college boy with the LSU hat. She looked him in the eyes and continued, "Sometimes, he took a young man, perhaps in the prime of his youth, without a care in the world. They say that Malick liked this flesh the most. This wet flesh. They say that it seared up best on the iron of his grill.

"But that is just what they say," Ella finished with a bit of a curtsy. The group clapped and cheered, some shaking the scare out of their shoulders.

Ella turned to lead the group back to the Alley. One more story left. The group was quieter now, probably thinking through how Malick chose his victims and what it would be like to be on one of those cargo ships that was stopped.

She raised her skirt and sheathed the silver knife. The gas lamp caught something else this time. LSU Hat gestured to his friend to look. He pointed to a tattoo of a white rabbit on the back of her upper thigh. A rabbit flying a kite.

# Nocturne

# Chapter 9
## New Orleans, Spring, Tuesday, 8:15ᵖᵐ

She did not like to swear, but there were limits. Sinclair was infuriating. He was just so goddamned distracted. Like clinically distracted. Was that a thing? She looked at Oliver and he looked back at her with his big dumb face. He gave her no advice and mostly seemed excited about the prospect of licking her nose.

She sat on the stoop of a shotgun house by the cross streets of Ursuline and Chartres. She had gotten to several of the tarot readers and she had talked to the old woman. There would be some cups in his future. She gave the old woman some baloney to eat in the hopes that this kindness would help her remember. But none of that mattered because he had decided that a strip club was the place to be tonight.

It was like when you had a so-so poker hand and you knew that you could still win with the cards you were dealt, but it was increasingly unlikely that you would win as the first three cards of the hand turned over on the table. She watched mule carts and ghost tours pass back and forth in front of her. It was quieter here, and not as many drunken people wandered by her on the step. So that was good. And it was cooler. Thank heavens for that.

She felt her internal clock ticking away and was not happy with her boy's behavior tonight. Not one bit.

She hoped the nudges she left would work.

But she wasn't optimistic.

# Chapter 10
# New Orleans, Spring, Tuesday, 8:15pm

We walk down Decatur and stop at one of the many frozen daiquiri shops. The flavors are ridiculous. There are like twenty flavors in all, set up in those swirling contraptions like they have at 7-Eleven. Banana Buttercup, Mardi Gras Grape, Hurricane's Eye, Peaches and Cream. I get a spiked lemonade. Dan is true to his word and slaps down the black AMEX and picks up the tab for us. Huck passes on the daiquiris, calling them vagina drinks. He tells us he'll get a beer like God intended man to drink. And don't be a fuck about the vagina drink comment, that's just Huck.

We cut down St. Louis toward Bourbon and Huck finds his drink. There's an older black man holding a sign that reads, "BIG ASS BEERS" and Huck is all about it.

"See, this is what I'm looking for, right here." Huck goes into the side shop, which is pretty much a counter stretched across an alleyway. A middle-aged man with a ponytail pulls on a tap next to a stack of four kegs.

The black man smiles and says, "You four need a picture under this beer sign, I think!" We slurp our drinks and agree with him. I give him a five and Dan takes out his phone and waits until Huck comes back with a large white cup filled with beer. It is indeed a big ass beer. Huck smiles and drinks deeply while we all take loud slurps of our daiquiris. We all smile and Dan takes the picture and posts it with the hashtags #boysnightout, #nobitches.

I smile. I'm sure they think, "Hey, what good guys we are and how cool it is that we are both helping our friend and screwing around on Bourbon Street at the same time. Look how happy Al is. We are good friends."

You want to know what I really am thinking? I suppose I can trust you. What I really think about is how is how that BITCH will feel tomorrow. And how it will be to sit in my dorm room overlooking the quad, looking at the pieces of her note in the trash. All about Chapter 2:15, "Strike adjacent to the object of your scorn and leave the pain that lasts for an eternity." Not that it matters, but I wonder if that would be enough to make her kill herself. The BITCH has tried several times before. Never serious attempts, just looking for attention. Typical for the Sneaky Snake Snatch. But I wonder if this will be the thing that finally puts her over the edge. Kind of gives me a half chub thinking about it. Thinking about her dead from pills or in a pool of blood.

I smile for another picture and pretend to take a drink from the spiked lemonade. That is something I have to be careful about. The last thing I need is to be drunk tonight. I walk a bit behind them and spill some out as we move towards Bourbon. Huck leads the crew and we hoot and holler down the street.

On either side of Bourbon, men and women throw beads down on the crowd from their balconies. Keith raises his shirt to a few of the ladies, displaying a rather impressive six-pack. Huh, good for him. Women toss beads at him while he tosses them back to us. He pulls his shorts down a bit and shows them his little happy trail. If you don't know, this is where they can almost see the top of his pubic hair. He does a little dance for them while women hoot and holler. They toss even more beads at him. One lets a feather boa fall slowly down into his waiting hands. He wraps it around his neck and blows them a kiss and says, "You're welcome." Soon, we look like everyone else on Bourbon, swaying to the music, beads hanging off our necks; looking to see how many of the deadly sins we can check off our list in one night.

Bunch of fucking rabble, if you ask me. They once had some kind of bullshit wrestling event here at the sports dome and it reminds me of that day. Fucking in-bred yokels carrying belts around like they won some kind of fight. A plague would do this city good.

We pass by another bar with a very chesty, short, fat woman out front with a collection of test tube shots. Her clothes are way too tight, goddamn fat pig. But I will say this, her tits are like these watermelon sized things. She catches Dan's eyes and puts one of the shots between her massive breasts and pulls him in close. Dan shrugs and puts his mouth on the tube, snuggling between those massive breasts like a prairie dog finding his home. Dan does this a number of times while we watch and pose for pictures. #boysnightout #nobitches

I am sure to smile in all of these pictures. Smiling with my drink in hand, now almost empty, as most of it was spilled on St. Louis leading to Bourbon. I take two of the empty test tubes and wave them around as well. Drunk Al, having the time of his life. All part of the plan. Chapter 3:4-5, "Choose wisely your path; be sly and clever, like the fox. Hunt, and forsake the howl." I cover my path. Which is easy, given the basic nature of Huck, Dan, and Keith. Idiots.

Keith leads us up to a fancier strip club called The Bayou. While the street is mostly filled with the indistinguishable rabble of Bourbon, I notice this tall guy in a Rolling Stones t-shirt who looks very familiar to me. I can't place him, but he reminds me of an academic or maybe a visiting lecturer in one of my classes. It's annoying. Anyway, he's arguing with a goofy looking drunk wearing a "Bourbon-Faced on Shit Street" t-shirt. I laugh at that. Novelty t-shirts amuse me.

Huck and Dan walk past me, missing the argument and focusing instead on this hot redhead piece of ass outside the club wearing a tight black bikini. Bourbon-Faced steps toward the older dude and seems to take a swing at him. He's clearly drunk and misses, falling off-balance, and his cigarette launches out of his hand a few feet to my left. The drunk tries to steady himself as he starts to go down by grabbing the nearest object. That nearest object is Huck. Specifically, it's Huck's beer-holding arm. The remaining beer spills all over Huck. Dan has this epic, kind of distant grin that comes across his face, like a dog that suddenly breaks free of a leash.

The beer cup goes flying into a nearby homeless man's cardboard sign and baseball cap, sending coins spilling onto the street. The old homeless man swats the cup away with a look of disdain and wipes beer off his notebook with a muffled swear. Dan gives this kick to the guy who spilled Huck's drink and calls him a drunk. Huck looks sadly at his lost beer. Dan gives the drunken guy another few kicks. The man huddles into a fetal position to protect his face. I see the bouncer, this massive guy who reminds me of Dr. Vin Diesel, starting to move toward the ruckus. A couple of guys wearing nice clothes start shouting at Dan to leave the drunk alone. Huck sees this as well and pulls Dan off the drunk guy on the ground.

Keith says, "Maybe this isn't the best club for us tonight. I know another one down the way. The girls are way more handsy." Dan puts his hands up in an "I ain't got no problem" manner and walks away from the bouncer. Bourbon-Faced groans and struggles to his feet. Mr. Rolling Stones is nowhere to be seen.

We walk further down Bourbon and find Huck another giant beer. We stop in a tequila bar and Dan teaches us all the proper way to have a tequila shot dressed with salt and lime. After two of these, I start thinking that I need to find a way to move somewhere else. I can hold my liquor, but getting drunk tonight isn't in the plans for me. I need somewhere that doesn't have my every shot watched.

"Hey Keith, you said there was a club a little further down with some handsy girls?" I ask.

Keith brightens at this and says, "Hell yeah! Come on." He pulls on Dan and Huck. "Let's get Al some pussy in his face."

Done. Fucking lemmings, these guys are.

Dan pays the bill again and I move up close to him the way I should and say, "Man, thanks for doing that. I'm already feeling like that BITCH is far behind me. You guys are good friends." Dan smiles at this and says back, "Of course man, we have to stick together. We've all been there before. You'll find another piece soon enough."

Keith and Huck are out ahead of us and I walk out with Dan. Keith leads us down two more blocks to a club called The Thang. The sign out front says, "LIVE SEX ACTS! ON STAGE!" Leave it to Keith to find this place. The girl at the front must be in her early 30s. She is wearing tight black shorts and a matching referee stripe shirt. She holds a large cardboard sign that says, "NO COVER, Two drink minimum."

The hallway into The Thang is short. There is a bar on the left and a bunch of seating with tables before it. There are three or four women in various styles of lingerie sitting on couches near the entrance in front of the bar. Dan orders us two beers each and starts a tab. The bartender, an older woman who looks like Mrs. Claus if she was addicted to meth and started doing tricks down at the local truck stop, stamps each of us to show we paid for our alcohol and are legit to be in the club. It's a little red kitty. I look at mine on the back of my hand.

Keith sidles right up to the stage. There is a brown-haired woman in her twenties dancing. In a vomit inducing show of crass sexuality, there is a bed on the back of the stage. The stripper dances seductively around the pole near the bed. Keith lays down some singles on the stage. She comes up to him and moves his two beers out of the way. Free of the obstruction, she wraps her legs around his head and pulls him close. Keith is like a kid in a candy shop. He stands up and motor-boats her smallish breasts.

Dan and Huck sit down a row back from the stage with me. We watch the stripper continue to rub herself all over Keith and drink our beers. I get up to go to the bathroom in the back and take my first beer with me. I slap Keith on the shoulder as I go by and notice another stripper in the back part of the room wearing a police officer outfit and pretending to handcuff an older man. I hear her cough as I walk by to the bathroom. Deep and contagious, like something that probably needs to be seen by a doctor quickly.

The bathroom doesn't have a door. There's one stall in the far corner and two urinals. The mirror seems to be made out of some kind of metal rather than glass. It has been scratched and graffitied up to the point where you can barely make yourself out in it, let alone make any cosmetic adjustments. I pour the beer down the sink and set the bottle on the shelf. I use the urinal.

"Pssst."

I freeze, the piss immediately stopping and my balls now clinging tight to me.

From the stall to my left, "Hey, kid. C'mere."

I zip up and then take the beer bottle in my hand. It's Mr. Conrad, the shark.

"Ya got that stick with you today? Big day. I know how much you like it. Swinging it around, poking at the lady and I, eh? And really, you earned it back, didn't you? Paid in full."

I back up without looking at the stall. I know what I'd see. The leathery skin and brilliant white teeth. I can hear the sound of him moving against the walls and his shoes shuffling on the floor. It's a small stall, so he doesn't fit well. His thick shoulders and biceps must bulge against the grey suit and slide against the narrow walls. He'd have on a blood red tie with a single pearl in the center.

But he is right. This is a big day. And I'm not going to be thrown off by this fuck. Not today. I walk out of the bathroom and hear him in a faint whisper, "Good luck there, kid. We'll be watching."

I sit down at one of the back tables to gather my thoughts before returning to Dan, Huck, and Keith. I try not to look around to see if Valentine is somewhere in the club. I can't handle that right now. The brown-haired girl is now sitting next to Keith and talking to him. Dan and Huck have moved up to the stage and are locked in a debate as another girl dances on stage around the pole. She has a rather large baby bump and what appear to be engorged and dark brown areolas peeking through her sheer bra.

A matching sheer fabric flows around her belly, doing a poor job of hiding her pregnancy.

"Hey, there," comes from behind me. I jump.

I panic and think its Valentine. I resist the urge to scream and take a deep breath and return to the good book, Chapter 8:7, "Leave the sharks to eat their dead."

It's just the words, not the voice. This calms me. It is the voice of an older woman, probably in her sixties, with big tits and leathery skin. She's dressed up in a nurse's outfit, with a white hat and a big red cross. I almost wish it was Valentine. Well, not really.

"Wanna see a trick?" she asks me and begins to fidget with her costume.

"Um, no thank you. I'm with some friends over there," I say and stand up to rejoin the guys.

"Suit yourself. It's a really good trick." She goes back to fidgeting with her costume.

I cross the club and pretend to take a long drag to finish off my already finished beer. I sit back down at my seat and watch Huck and Dan continue their debate in front of the pregnant stripper. Keith walks to the back of the club with his new friend for an extended lap dance. He high-fives Dan as he goes by. Like it's a challenge to get a stripper to strip for you when you give her money.

I look around. The club is about half full, a mix of tourists and locals hanging out. There are still two or three strippers sitting on the couches by the door. The music is 80s hair band metal that is starting to grate on my nerves. I get up and head over to strung-out

Mrs. Claus and order three double whiskey shots and a half coke/half club soda. She asks if I want it on my friend's tab and I decline and set down a twenty and ten. She takes the money and gives me back my change in singles. I leave her a few ones and walk the drinks over to Dan and Keith.

The pregnant dancer moves over to stage left, closer to the back of the club. Dan and Keith step back from the stage, each finishing off their second beer. I put whiskey shots in front of each of them. I tell them, "You guys are the best!" over the loud club music. They smile back and take their whiskey and toast me. My smile is very genuine. I drink down the mixture of coke and club soda. My thoughts wander to what will happen later. How it is going to feel. My smile gets even bigger at this thought. Don't be a fuck about it. Just give me this minute to myself. I lean back and smile. Cheshire cat.

There is a slow clapping that starts with a group of beaded girls in the front of the club. Several others join in the clapping. The older stripper in the nurse's outfit takes the stage. It isn't a pretty sight, I can tell you that. I turn back to Dan and Huck.

"What were you two talking about up there?" I ask, pointing to the girl on the back end of the stage partially blocked by the elder nurse. The pregnant dancer found a black man with his white girlfriend to dance in front of and she is currently slapping her full breasts back and forth in the girl's face while her man claps his hands and leans back to take it all in.

Dan points at Huck, "This dumb-ass didn't know that she was pregnant. He just thought that she was a big girl."

Huck defends himself and says, "Who would get up there and dance while she's pregnant, man? There is no way. No one is that sketchy."

Dan laughs and says, "See! Come on man. She's a damned stripper. She isn't making good, safe choices in her life. Hey, maybe you could ask her for a dance and see if she would give you a discount on a threesome!" Dan laughs loudly at this.

Huck drinks his whiskey and shakes his head. I'm just happy they're both drinking heavily. On stage, the nurse takes out one of her breasts as some Whitesnake ballad blares over the bad sound system. The crowd starts to clap as she takes out her other breast and I can see what seem to be two wooden matches in the piercing holes of her nipples. Without missing a beat, she lights the first match and then the second. The crowd claps loudly and she dances about, saluting those who are throwing dollar bills at her.

As she puts out the fire on her breasts, Keith walks back with his new stripper friend looking a bit disheveled after their private lap dance. He sits down in front of his second beer and whiskey. He drinks the whiskey down and takes the beer as a chaser.

"Good dance?" Dan asks him as the nurse moves to the second stage position and the pregnant dancer steps down. A tall, too-thin bald girl with more tattoos than I have ever seen on one person takes the stage.

Keith smiles back and says, "Fuck yeah!"

Huck says, "Hey, I need some food. You guys willing to hit another club and grab something on the way?" He looks over to me, "Unless Al here wants a dance with the nurse."

I'm tired of all of this. Cover story or no, it's time to move them along. I laugh and say, "Ha. Even I'm not that heartbroken. I could totally use a hotdog and a new club."

Dan pays the tab on the way out. We walk out onto Bourbon and across the street is a Lucky Dog cart. We order four with the works and then get some beers from another nearby bar window. I take a bite of the hotdog and enjoy the taste. I know I will need this energy later. I take a slow swig on the beer and begin the process of letting it spill as we walk down the street.

"Hey, let's try that Bayou place again. It's my favorite," Keith says.

We nod in unison and walk up the steps to The Bayou. The redhead in the black bikini has been replaced by an athletic black girl in a neon pink fishnet outfit. The muscled bouncer is still outside. He seems to have let bygones be bygones and allows us in the club. Dan pays a five-dollar cover for each of us. The bouncer adds a black sharpie B to our hands above the red kitty. I suggest Dan take a picture. He obliges. Four men on the town for a boys' night. He convinces the stripper out front in the fishnet outfit to get into the picture with us and then posts it. #boysnightout #nobitches

This club couldn't be any more different than the last place. The bar is long, sleek, and black, and currently being tended by a fancy guy in a black t-shirt and dark hair. Where the other club blasted 80s hair band rock, here the music is electronica with thumping bass throughout that seems to make every surface in the place vibrate. I will give this to Keith: he does know how to pick a strip club. This one is packed with people compared to the last. There must be a dozen dancers mixed in with the businessmen, bachelor party guys, and a remarkable number of couples and women. I guess the times are changing for the lesbian chic. Whole goddamn city is a Sodom and Gomorrah. Lubricate them Sodomites up with some napalm. I laugh at this. Don't be a fuck about it.

As we wait at the bar, we realize the place is too packed to have the bartender even notice us. Where beer was the main drink at the last, ramshackle place, this guy is working the cocktail stick and shaker at a top-shelf pace. After I see him make the third martini, the charm of his bartending skills begins to fade. Dan pulls us over to a table near the right side of the stage to sit down. He points to a waitress with blue, short hair in a corset top, black hot pants, and fishnet stockings, who seems to be taking drink orders from around the club.

Next to us are four large black men with two strippers sitting at their table. There is a lot of "Hey honey, come sit here on my lap, I'll be your black Santa Claus," and ample touching as the women lean in and whisper god knows what to the men. We settle in and smile and watch the thin girl on stage with the angel wing tattoos do some impressive pole work. Another stripper is at the stage with a group of college guys and women waving dollar bills. She reaches up from her seat and kisses the stripper on stage full on the mouth and slips a five in her G-string. The crowd loves it and hoots and claps their appreciation.

"What'll it be?" the waitress asks us. Dan orders a round of crown and cokes for the table and some tequila shots. He slips the waitress his credit card to a round of back slapping from Huck, Keith, and me.

Two girls come over to our table and start talking up Huck and Dan. The DJ, set somewhere high up and in the back of the club, says, "Let's hear it for Mercedes! All you cheap bastards out there put your hands together!" Huck and Dan talk to their new lady friends and Keith taps me on the arm all excited.

"Oh, man. You are gonna love this next girl. She is amazing." Keith gestures to a tall woman in a black dress, slim and sleek, deeply cut. He's right, this girl is in another league compared to the ones from the last club. More like another species.

Keith moves up to the stage and leaves me with Dan and Huck. Huck's girl, short and Asian, climbs up in his lap like some kind of cat. Dan is leaning in and talking into his girl's ear. Keith is eagerly sitting at the stage like a kid at a carnival show. The DJ announces, "Let's give it up for Cassandra!!!"

The music switches over to a slow and seductive techno beat. Something like the Cure meets Depeche Mode, kind of hypnotic and dark. Cassandra starts to dance. She is exotic and much taller than the last dancer. She reminds me of how a snake slides and slithers. She has a simple silver locket that hangs between her breasts that catches my eye. I give props again to Keith; he knows his strippers.

Our waitress returns with our drinks and, at my direction, walks over to Keith to bring him his cocktail and shot. I take the chance to pick up my shot and hold it in my hand and turn away from Dan and Huck to watch Cassandra slink across the stage. I start to let the shot spill to the floor under the table, likely adding to any variety of unknown liquids spilled in this place.

"Careful there," comes from my side, "you are spilling your drink. Though, Cassandra has that effect on a lot of people." I turn to see the redhead from earlier in the black bikini standing above me.

"Mind if I sit?" she asks. Then suddenly I have her on my lap. "My name is Mynx. What's yours?" She snuggles up against my chest.

"I'm Al, nice to meet you Mynx." I set down my empty shot glass on the table, unnoticed by Huck and Dan, and take a sip of the crown and coke.

She asks all the normal questions. Are you local? You go to school? What do you study? Oh, I studied something like that too. The music switches over from the seductive sexy into something a bit more Nine Inch Nails meets Lovage. Cassandra moves into her second set. Huck takes his little Asian treat to one of the back rooms for a dance. Dan seems enthralled in a conversation. I hold up my end of the conversation with Mynx and spend the appropriate amount of time staring at her ample cleavage.

I don't want you to think I don't like girls. I like girls. So, don't be a fuck about it. What I struggle with is this vapid ball of fluff on my lap and the likely amount of diseases that are cycling in her bloodstream and in her dirty holes. But, this was always part of the plan.

"Hey so, Mynx, want to go and have a dance with me in the back?" I ask her. She smiles back at me with a wink and says, "You know I do," as she gets up and walks me back to the VIP section. Dan and Huck high-five me as I go. "Go get some, Al!" and "Hell ya, playa. Forget that other ho," follow me to the back.

Cassandra finishes her dance on the stage as we walk by. Mynx has my hand and brings me to a desk before the door leading outside. The short, heavy-set man behind the desk working the register wears a grey bowler hat with a black stripe. "What'll it be?" he asks us both, but mostly Mynx. She looks to me. She says, "It's one dance for $40 in the back room and three for a hundred." I say, "Maybe let's just start with one and see how it goes from there." She smiles at me without missing a beat and turns to Bowler Hat. "Just one to start," she says. "I'll see if I can convince him to get some more when we get back in the dark. I can be very persuasive." I take out two twenties and leave them on the desk. Bowler makes change and pushes back a ten and twenty to Mynx. She makes the money disappear into her black clutch. It has a neon pink kitty on it.

She guides me out of the club and down a short courtyard that has small rooms on the left side of the building and a fountain with chairs around it on the right. She leads me to the first room, where the sound from the main club is being pumped in via a speaker in the ceiling. Mynx pulls my hand and I follow her in. "Get comfortable, handsome," she says, sitting me in the center of a couch in the back of the room and setting her purse on the table before taking off her stiletto heels.

I'll spare you the details of the dance. They are unremarkable. My goal here is not to get off with some nasty whore, but rather show the guys I'm taking some time to enjoy myself and to be in a club where I can disappear for a while. Mynx takes off her top, grinds a bit on me, and then the song is over. Under three minutes. She makes a push to upsell me for some more dances, but I think she gets that I'm not overly interested in her. No lead in the pencil, so to speak. Well, no lead for her. That's for later.

She leads me out and I return an awkward hug with her while she excuses herself to go to the restroom. I see Keith talking with Cassandra in the corner, likely negotiating a marriage proposal. Dan and Huck are back at the table with their respective girls. They order drinks from the waitress.

It's time for me to make my move. I walk over to the bar and confirm that they are all distracted. If anything, the club has gotten busier. I give the club one more sweep—all clear with my friends—and walk out onto the street.

The air feels different. Kind of an electricity in the night. I walk back to my car, parked over in the lot by Decatur. It's a quick walk to the Chevy Impala, parked on the far side of the lot without the security cameras looking over me.

I unlock the trunk and sling the black cape over one shoulder. It's a bit warm, but it's important for all my fun. There is a nice hood sewn into the fabric as well. I take out the large pack and sling it onto my back. It's heavy with the P90, Glock, tactical vest, body armor, and extra clips. There is also my mask. I'm very excited to wear that mask.

I carry out the three bags from Rouses shopping market. They are cloth bags, each weighed down with what looks like 2–3 lbs. of groceries. Two of them contain Huck's M-80 fireworks rigged to some fuses and modified soda bottles. The last bag contains my best impression of what a bomb would look like to a regular person. Wires, LED lights, and batteries with duct tape wrapped around a pipe. In the end, this one has nothing but some gun powder from one of the M-80's sprinkled on the outside and the leavings from a few sparklers scraped into the bottom of the bag. Not anything that would do any damage, but it sure looks concerning. About 30 minutes of concerning. All the bags have light items like potato chips and paper towels on the top.

Chapter 5:5, "Check the bolts securing the grand Ferris wheel to the earth, as once the spinning starts, an ounce of prevention is worth a pound of cure." Everything is squared and verified. I'm ready.

Despite the heavy load, I walk with a spring in my step.

It's time to start the show.

Time for the thunder.

# Chapter 11
## New Orleans, Spring, Tuesday, 8:15<sup>pm</sup>

The night spun Wagner onto Bourbon Street. The alcohol from the four quick drinks continued to fuel a nice buzz as he walked into the crowd. There was electricity in the air. The sights and sounds blended together. They called him deeper down Bourbon Street.

Wagner was out of sorts. He was annoyed and frustrated at having left Cassandra. He felt this growing weariness coming over him with everything going on today.  Hell, maybe Cassandra was the person he was supposed to meet in the bar. But he knew that wasn't right. Not by a long shot.

In his distraction, he walked directly into a thin, wiry man with dirty brown hair. He wore a faded t-shirt with the words, "I got Bourbon-Faced on Shit Street" printed across the front. He wore jeans that carried their own story of stains and rips from his travels. He held a cigarette in one hand and a half-filled plastic cup with the logo of Hurricane Joe's in the other. Wagner pushed past him.

"Heeeeeyyyy!" he said.

Wagner turned back and looked at him.

"So that's your how-do-you-do? Not even a hello? Nothing?" He wove back and forth in time to the music blasting out of the club across the street.

Wagner looked him over. He wasn't the least bit familiar to him. "I'm sorry, do I know you?" he said.

Bourbon-Faced feigned a look of surprise and shock at Wagner's words. "Do you…do you know…KNOW ME?" He brought his hand down hard against his chest. "That hurts, man. Hurts right here." He pounded his chest in case Wagner didn't get the reference.

"I'm sorry…I just don't think…" Wagner began. The man attempted to playfully punch Wagner in the arm and succeeded in missing the arm all together and instead lost both his cigarette and drink all at once. He spun and went down and crashed onto the street. In his fall, he tried to catch himself by grabbing onto a group of young college students, one lanky and tall wearing a green wave t-shirt and holding an unrealistically large white cup with the words Huge Ass Beer on the front. Another had an opossum on his shirt and a third looked at Wagner with alert eyes. He was wearing black jeans and had some kind of fox on his shirt.

The drink spilled on Green-Wave T-Shirt and Opossum Kid got this shit-eating grin on his face. He instinctively kicked at Bourbon-Faced as he fell to the ground. The Huge Ass Beer hit the ground in a splash. Green-Wave T-Shirt looked sadly at his beer, as if amazed that it was truly gone. Coins spilled onto the street, probably from the pockets of one of the kids. Opossum Kid continued to kick at the man on the ground. The tall, lanky kid seemed to come to his senses and tried to pull his friend off Bourbon-Faced as the kicking intensified.

Opossum Kid yelled, "You goddamned drunk!" and kicked at him harder. Some well-dressed conventioneers yelled at the pair of college boys, "Hey! Leave him alone!" Others stopped and gawked. The bouncer took notice and went over to investigate.

Enough of this, Wagner thought. Another crazy night in the Quarter. The people on Bourbon swarmed around them and Wagner made his escape down the street. He thought of Mancuso arresting the elderly communist at the start of Toole's classic, *A Confederacy of Dunces*. The crowd formed, and Wagner-Ignatius made his escape in the chaos.

A man walked up to him, short and fat, and told Wagner excitedly, "Betcha I can tell ya where ya got dem shoes, big man!"

 Wagner avoided eye contact and told the man, "On my feet, my brother, right here in New Orleans..." and walked away. The scam was for tourists, with the hustler betting he could guess where you got your shoes. Jokes on you, though, you got your shoes on your feet, hee-haw!

The gas street lamps were on, most built and installed by the Bevolo Company around the corner on Royal Street. The lights flickered against the copper and glass and cast an eerie glow on the brick walls. There was a homeless woman coming toward him. She pushed a folding shopping cart filled to the brim with random items from the city. There was nothing worth anything much, but not totally worthless. An old baseball cap, an umbrella with broken spokes, a beat up red Igloo ice cooler, a bag of lighters, three large flashlights tied together, and a small rolling suitcase with a crushed end.

"Don't tell me to get out!" she yelled at no one in particular.

Wagner avoided eye contact and looked down at the street. She was about thirty feet in front of him. He considered switching to the other side of the block to avoid her. A premonition of sorts.

She muttered to herself, "I hate China in my brain layer. China is going to kill you. He forgot to die. Do you understand that? He forgot to die."

Buzzed and out of sorts, Wagner didn't really want to interact with this woman. His steps brought him closer though. Should he cross the street? Turn around? He kept walking toward her.

She didn't see him yet and continued to yell, "It was 16 weeks ago they came into my house and ate my groceries. That goddamn monkey president. Fuck Obama and his Mama!"

Wagner was close enough now to see that she was wearing a "walk for recovery" t-shirt. It was ripped and stained, and several sizes too large.

A plane flew above and she looked up at the blinking red lights as it crossed the sky. Wagner hoped this was enough to distract her so he could pass by without conversation.

"You see that? A flying bird on one finger." She shook her fist up at the plane as it crossed above her. "Don't be so greedy with the sky."

Wagner was too close now. She saw him and asked, "Do you think it will explode like the other one? Will it explode in the air?"

He tried to avoid her gaze and kept walking. New Orleans was always filled with characters, but this had been an exceptionally challenging day.

She wasn't hampered. "I see you...cheers to me, cheers to you. If you do, fuck you."

She reached into her cart and took out a plastic bag of baloney. She peeled off a piece and folded it twice before cramming it all into her mouth. She did the same again with a second slice. Wagner slowed as he passed her, mesmerized by her chewing. Like how cars slow as they pass the scene of an accident. A fascinating bit of mastication.

Bits of meat sprayed from her mouth as she spoke to Wagner, "It's a dark, dark day. I've sinned and we are not going to be able to get a move. It will be a cross next time. That will be the son of God."

She continued, "He was riding me. Riding all over me. He hears me now. Breaking my bones." She shook a piece of unfolded baloney at him for emphasis.

Wagner had enough. He picked up his pace. She called to him as he walked by, "The Rosary. You know she loves you no matter what! If you ever even had a momma. She is the greatest momma you never had. And she ain't no goddamn beggar."

She was mostly out of earshot now. Wagner quickened his pace.

"No one would die for you!" she yelled in a high-pitched screech.

Wagner turned back to her. Something about what she was yelling. That same elusive feeling. Just hovering at the distant limits of his memory. Familiar but forgotten.

"You know that, right? No one would die for you! You are empty!"

He walked away from her and towards Jackson Square.

There was a light wind cutting through the night. He wished he'd worn a heavier shirt. His apartment wasn't far down from Jackson, toward the Marigny and Bywater, adjacent to the Quarter. A group of musicians formed a band of sorts and blared out the classics, like "When the Saints go Marching In", and "St. James Infirmary Blues" to throngs of tourists huddled against the ramparts of the cathedral.

Scattered among the musicians and the homeless attempting to stretch out on the benches was an assortment of fortunetellers, oracles, and tarot readers. A woman in a long peasant dress with violet streaks woven into her hair caught Wagner's eye and invited him to sit down.

Normally, he would have kept walking, but this day had already been far from normal. Maybe some guidance from the other side would help ease his mind.

"My name is Jade. Would you like to know your future?" she asked Wagner.

Jade was in her late forties and had the look of someone who has lived close to the streets. Not homeless—always a few steps away from that—but not that many steps.

"I'm Wagner. Nice to meet you. I feel like some clarity is just what I need in my life tonight," he said.

Jade shuffled the cards and placed a golf-ball sized piece of clear crystal on top of the deck.

She gestured to Wagner. "You cut the deck."

Wagner obliged and split the deck near the middle. Jade took the cards and laid them out, three cards in front of him face down.

"You're local, of course?" Jade said.

"Yes, fairly local," Wagner replied.

Locals had a certain way about them that differentiated them from the tourists. To a practiced eye, something as simple as the shoes you wore could tell the entire story. The way people dressed, how they crossed a street, all of it tells a story about where you are from, how often you visit. Before moving down from Boston, Wagner had come to New Orleans each month to write. By the eighth or ninth trip, people assumed he was local. No magic fortune telling here, not yet.

"Let's see. The first tells of your past. Where you have been and who you are." She flipped the card.

Wagner looked at a seated man in a chariot with a wand in his right hand. He sat between two sphinxes, one black and one white. Castles rose in the background of the card and there was a cloth with stars draped over the chariot. The numeral VII stood above the seated man at the top of the card.

"The chariot. Two cats, one black and one white. You are a person of dichotomies," she said.

"In the past, you had a sense of focus and determination in reaching your goals. You had confidence in your abilities. Boldness to the point of aggression in your endeavors." She looked up to him.

Wagner nodded politely. He was captivated by the two figures at the bottom of the card. The sphinxes.

"Good and evil. You've been through battles and choices. And have come through with a firm stance and perseverance."

Wagner nodded again, not giving much away to Jade, and thanked her for her interpretation. He had read some about the tarot, dabbled in it some himself even. He had a deck that sat on his bookshelf between Sartre and Faulkner, this time Faulkner's *Sound and Fury,* not his cat.

Jade smiled, "I see your determination from the past. It still clings. Let's see what your current situation is." She reached for the middle card.

Wagner's eyes widened at the turning of the card. The tower. It's rare to draw two cards from the major arcana, let alone this particular card given his day's events. The major arcana is made up of 22 cards, with the remaining 56 cards of the deck called the minor arcana. These were then further divided into four suits of 14 cards each: cups, wands, pentacles, and swords. Emotions, passion and ideas, material possessions, and challenges within you, roughly translated.

The card was dark, with a gray-stone tower in the center and people falling from either side as lightning and fire exploded at the apex. Clouds floated and small wisps of fire poured from the windows. By any stretch of the imagination, it was an ominous card.

Jade ran her finger over the card. "There is conflict in your life. An unexpected event has recently disturbed you. Given the context of the first card you drew, your ambition and success may have been built on a false premise. It is time for a change." She looked at Wagner.

"While you may feel shaken and disturbed, these are normal reactions to a tower event. But with the destruction and instability, there comes a salvation. The last card will give you a clue as to how you will see your way through the event that has disturbed your peace and harmony. This next card is your salvation. It is your way out."

She turned the last card. A man stood in a boat and held a long pole while he guided the boat across a river. Six swords stood upright in the boat. A crouched and hooded female figure sat next to a little boy in the center of the boat. The shore was far off in the distance. The waves were turbulent in the foreground, almost as if the boat had come through some rapids. The water was flat and smooth in front of the boat. The numeral VI was etched at the top.

Jade smiled at this card and made a happy sigh "Ahhhhh. This is a good card for you. While the journey has been hard, the path forward is clear. You have success waiting for you ahead on the opposite shore. You will overcome the obstacles in front of you. You will help the girl."

"What?" Wagner asked.

"There is a girl. She is on your journey as well." Jade touched the cloaked figure. "She in turn helped the boy. The cloak hid her from the world. She was often mysterious and unknown. An aspiration of sorts."

This revelation was too close to the truth for Wagner. Jade saw the concern in his eyes and looked thoughtfully at the deck. She touched the crystal for guidance. Jade said, "I feel like the deck has something else to tell you. May I turn over some other cards?"

Wagner's mouth was dry and he swallowed. That foggy feeling was back. Not quite déjà vu, but something like it. He nodded wordlessly to Jade and she shuffled the deck again, carefully mixing the cards five or six times. She asked Wagner to cut the deck. He obliged.

Jade set down three more cards in a row and turned them over in rapid succession. Cups. The Ace of Cups, the Two of Cups, the Three of Cups. Now it was Jade who looked shaken up. A cup overflowing with water. Two figures holding cups between an angel. Three women holding cups. People drinking. Cups overflowing.

"That's very, very odd. To draw three of the same suit. And to draw them in order. So many cups lined up at once. This is important for you. An emphasis." Jade nodded to herself.

Wagner felt a sense of dread growing again. Somewhere deep. Something broken and pinballing against the machine.

She shuffled the deck once more. This time, eight or nine cycles, she shuffled the cards quickly in her hands. She cut the deck first this time. She cut it once and then she cut the deck again. She then had Wagner cut the deck one last time and drew three more cards.

Four of Cups. Five of Cups. Six of Cups.

The odds were astronomical. A man sat on the ground surrounded by cups. A dark figure holding a cup. Children playing by cups.

Jade tried some humor. "So many cups. And all in order. A powerful message for you. Perhaps with all these cups, you are to open a bar in your future?"

Wagner fumbled to take a twenty out of his front pocket and stepped back from the table.

"Thank you," he said in a soft voice. His legs swayed.

Jade nodded, mesmerized by the cards. She shuffled the deck again as Wagner left her. She thought for a moment that she should try to help calm him. The mysteries of the cards can unnerve, and there are many ways to interpret how they fall. Still. She finished shuffling and the next cards came up. She did what the girl had asked, but these cards fell of their own accord.

Seven, Eight, Nine of cups.

The nine was an image of a seated man. A tall bar stretched out behind him and a stack of nine golden cups sat on the bar. The nine of cups, a card of abundance. Wine to drink or cups to sell.

So many cards ordered exactly in succession spooked Jade deeply, and she was not one to frighten easily. Something bigger was happening here. Perhaps it was that girl and her dog that had spooked her earlier. There was something about that one she found disquieting. Jade decided to pack up for the night. She shuffled the deck together and put her crystals and tarot cards in her knapsack and packed her table and chairs.

She watched the fading figure of Wagner cross St. Ann by the square in front of Muriel's restaurant. She thought of the ghost of Pierre Antoine Lepardi Jourdan, said to haunt the building after committing suicide on the second floor after losing the lease in an ill-fated card game. They set a table for him each night in the very back of the building. Maybe that was a good omen for her customer to open a bar. Maybe that path will hold some salvation for him.

She finished packing and walked across the darkened square.

# Chapter 12
## New Orleans, Spring, Tuesday, 8:15ᵖᵐ

Ella led the group back down Chartres for their last ghost story. She liked to tell it down Pere Antoine Alley by Jackson Square and the St. Louis Cathedral. It was rarely busy down the alley. It had a comforting, closed-in feeling with a large tour group. Sometimes, when she was doing tours at the same time as Dave, they would meet up here and really pack the group in.

"Careful here, avoid stepping in the rain gutter. You wouldn't want to trip or lose your balance," Ella warned the group about the long, cut trench that broke up the cobblestones in the center of the street. Two of the children stepped over it and looked carefully at the stone, so foreign from their own home's pavement and blacktop. That was part of the allure of New Orleans, like stepping into history. Ella knew this was what most of Europe looked like, so stepping back a few hundred years was nothing compared to the castles and roads she had seen during her travels abroad.

"So, you've survived the night so far; which is good. That's what many people feel as they walk around the city at night. Perhaps you've heard these stories as well if you are visiting from afar. The city is safe, but best to keep to the center of the Quarter. Wander too far on the outskirts and the city starts to get a little thinner, a little more dangerous." Ella surveyed the group. The Brittney's Bitches were out of alcohol. She guessed they would be the first to line back up at the bar.

"See, that's what people thought. That it was safe here. But they were wrong. No one was safe from Marauding Jack. A few of you might be old enough to remember the stories from the 50s. This is when the murders occurred." She looked around to see some of the older tour members nod in agreement.

"Some say they called him Jack out of homage to the famous murderer Jack the Ripper from the late 1800s. There are similarities, of course, since both killers preferred to be all up close and personal-like with a knife. Jack the Ripper preyed on prostitutes and women of the night, while Marauding Jack was a little less picky. Jack the Ripper focused on the Whitechapel district of London, while Marauding Jack was drawn to the French Quarter of New Orleans.

"The murders here occurred over the summer in 1951. Ten were killed when all was said and done. There were six women and four men, three of whom were well-to-do socialites or business people. The other seven came from various lesser backgrounds, including three homeless. Some were local to the city, some visitors. The police spent a long time trying to find a pattern in the killings, but never got close to understanding the mind of Marauding Jack.

"What makes this story interesting is the one victim of Jack's knife who lived—a young girl named Adaline de Croix. She met Jack and received no less than 15 stab wounds from him. He left her here, right in this very alley, to die. But Jack may have made his first mistake by choosing this alley. Perhaps it was the ghost of

Antonio de Sedella, a Spanish friar who took part in the Inquisitions and who baptized the famous Voodoo priestess Marie Laveau. Perhaps it was the more public location of the attempted killing next to the church. It is hard to say. But Adaline lived, and lives to this day as a caretaker in the Old Ursuline Convent Museum. She has never spoken of the attack. Some wonder if it was the terror of that night or the damage to her vocal chords, but she hasn't spoken a word since."

Ella paused here and took a different tone with the group. "I'm sure you're asking yourself why I'm telling you this story. This is a ghost tour. This is not a tour of famous historical killers and murders in the city; though, there have been many of those." Ella saw the nods from the group. They waited for her next words. "You see, the murders stopped, but the stories continue to this day. They say when something so horrific occurs on holy ground, it creates a grounding place for the otherworldly. To this day, people tell stories of experiencing sudden chills when they walk this street and feelings of vertigo when they stand on the spot where young Miss de Croix bled so much on the cobblestone.

"Jack would be in his 80s today if he was a young man when he started his killing. Quite a bit older, if he had reached mid-age before he carried out his macabre plan. I think he had filled his gullet with the killings and went into his old age and death, holding onto the memories of those he killed. Some think that when he died, the ghost of Antonio de Sedella drew him back to this place in the city. Perhaps the ghost took it personally that Jack chose this alley, his final resting place, to draw blood. Or it could be the ghost of de Sedalla hadn't gotten enough torture during the Spanish Inquisition to satiate his appetite. Perhaps he was looking for a soul to purify for Christ.

"No one knows for sure. But they do say that if you stand here, right here next to where I'm standing, in the very place where the blood of Miss Adaline de Croix pooled almost seventy years ago on an evening much like this, that maybe you will feel something." The group quietly looked down at the length of rain gutter with wide eyes.

Ella continued, "I don't stand on that spot anymore. I am careful to avoid it. I even warn others about crossing it." Ella looked to the young children who crossed it earlier and then backed away from the spot toward Royal Street.

She gave one more admonition to the group, "If you are brave enough, or foolish enough, perhaps you will stand there. Maybe just for a brief moment to think about Miss de Croix, lying on the cobblestones as she watched her blood flow out and away from her. Perhaps you will feel that sudden chill or dizziness that so many have felt before. Maybe, if you were to kneel down and look back towards Jackson Square, much like she did, you will feel her, struggling to breathe, braced by horrific pain, watching Marauding Jack stride away from her, into the night."

The group took turns and gathered around the spot Ella had indicated. She watched some kneel down and stand back up; sometimes they were creeped out, sometimes they just stepped back and shook their heads in disappointment. It looked as if one blonde in Brittney's Bash actually flashed the spot and called out to the ghost to come get some. Nice. Sigh.

Peg-Leg Pete's and Ghost Alley Tours was just around the block. Ella brought the group back there to complete their tour. Liv wasn't at her post, which was strange. She wondered where she was. Cliff was telling a story to a group of people by the Crow's Nest. The bar was extremely full; the late-night tour always drew larger crowds. She elbowed her way past several thirsty people and set down her bottle for Hope to fill. She gave her a wink and said, "thirsty work." Hope had a tall woman with a small dog on the hook for three cannonball shots. The  dog was currently licking the ice glass in her hand before she threw it at the wall.

The gift shop and bar usually did some brisk business right after the tour. A few of them slipped Ella tens and fives as tips for a good tour. As she predicted, LSU Hat handed her a piece of paper with his number and, pleasantly, a $10 bill. She gave him a gracious smile as one of Brittney's Bitches pulled her aside and thanked her for the tour with a too-happy, California "so much!" She slipped a twenty into her hand. She said, "It just made Brittney's night. I'm her maid of honor and I'm so glad I booked this here with you. I'll totally give you a good review on my phone!" Ella noticed a newcomer to the bar over the maid of honor's shoulder. He was Caucasian and tall, with a thin build, in his early thirties and wearing jeans, black boots, and a black leather jacket. His hair fell around his eyes, although Ella could still see their steel blue looking back at her with a smile. She broke free from Brittney's maid of honor with a thank you and walked over to him.

"Coop!" she said and gave him a long hug. He hugged her back and said, "Hey there, baby."

"You ready for tonight?" she asked him, regretfully breaking away from the hug. He felt good. She could have lingered there all night.

"I think so. It's a new set, so we still have some kinks to work out. But you know, that's just rock and roll; it isn't always clean. How was your first tour?" he asked.

"Oh, I killed it with this group. Bachelorette party. Hey, come with me in the back. I wanna hear about the new set. Do you have a few?"

"Sure, I don't meet up with them till a little after 9," he said and took her hand as they walked back past the bar. Ella took her bottle of beer from Hope with a "thank you," and they went into the staff lounge. Dave was again sitting at the computer and playing solitaire. He looked up and said, "Hey Cooper. Good to see you." Coop waved back and sat down at a couch in the corner of the room. Ella tossed the piece of paper LSU Hat had given her in the half-filled bowl.

"Tour go okay, Dave?" Ella asked him.

"Hey! Sweet," he said at the paper in the bowl. "So many horny men out there needing a lesson." Then back to Ella, "The tour was pretty good. Kid got sick about halfway through and left a pretty good mess on the street. Not that anyone will notice in the Quarter."

"I killed with Malick tonight. Really freaked some people out." She intertwined her fingers between Coops like she was in high school. He had that effect on her. Rockstar boyfriend.

"See, it's that knife bit you do." Dave brightened some. "Hey, mind if we meet up for the last group? I'll swap stories and you can do Malick for both groups?"

Ella thought. She did like that bit and having an audience. "Well…"

"Come on, it'll be great! Meet you at 10 at Bourbon and Dauphine. We can walk them back and split at the blacksmith shop so you can do Jack in the alley. I haven't seen you do Malick in a while. You always give me chills with that one."

"Okay, okay. But do me a favor; let Coop and I talk for a bit? Do you mind?" she asked Dave. "Done!" Dave stood up and packed up his things, Zazu bobbing up and down. "This makes the night go by so much faster." He clicked over to the schedule on the computer. "Big group tonight, too. Check it out when you get a chance. Full boat. "

Dave crossed the room and gave Ella a high-five. "Rock it out tonight," he said to Cooper as he walked through the door.

"Dave, have you seen Liv?" Ella asked, but the door had already swung shut.

"Look at you, tour guide extraordinaire," Coop said. She smiled. She stood up and walked to the door and slid the dead bolt into place.

She took a deep swig of beer and hovered over Coop on the couch. She handed him the bottle. He took a drink.

Ella raised her skirt and straddled him, "So, Mr. Rockstar. Do you want to tell me about your set?" She took the bottle from him, had a long pull on it, and set it down on the table next to the couch. She could feel him growing hard against her through his jeans.

"Well, I think we're going to open with…" She kissed him, ending his sentence in a muffled surprise noise. He had the taste of gin on his lips and her tongue went deeper, pressing into his mouth. Her grey-white hair fell across her face as he worked to undo her top. Ella ran her fingers through his hair and then scraped her nails against his shoulders. She placed his hands on her hips and he kissed her harder.

On the other side of the bolted door, a cannonball shot glass shattered against the wall. They startled at this and then chuckled, accompanied by shouts and laughter from the bar. She brushed the hair out of his face and kissed him more gently. His hands were an effortless blur, roving across her body.

The two were alone in the world, the silver knife handle glistening, sheathed on Ella's outer thigh. Captain Malick and Pirate Alley Ghost Tours were far from their minds.

# Crescendo

# Chapter 13
## New Orleans, Spring, Tuesday, 9:45ᴘᴍ

ell, shit. She knew it was too late. That old Abba song went through her head. What was it again? The name came to her. "Winner Takes It All." No more ace to play.

She waited and looked at a balcony above her with a brightly lit metal tree. The lights were all purple and shimmering. She liked the way they called out into the night. Like a million little fairies. All hovering in one place.

She stroked Oliver on his head and down his long back while she waited some more. She ran over the day and thought about what else she could have done. She supposed she could have held him down and hit him until he understood. But that wasn't the way, she had been told.

She waited until she heard the loud thud from several blocks away up towards Canal Street. That was the start. It sounded like

134

someone had struck a loud gong in a hollow dumpster. Minutes later, she could hear the distant sirens start. It wouldn't be long now.

The second explosive thud occurred closer to Decatur and the river's edge. Like thunder over the water. The sirens were louder now. She imagined the fire trucks and police swarming to the location of the detonation. She'd seen it before, so she didn't need to really use her imagination.

She waited again, stroking Oliver and calming him when the familiar staccato pop, pop, pop of rifle fire sounded from a block behind her. Then the screams. More pop, pop, pop. More screams.

The sirens were now loud and echoing all around the Quarter. It was like they had set up the world's best hi-fi system to blast out the worst songs.

Well, shit.

She stood up and headed over to the Crescent City Grille.

Oliver padded along behind her.

# Chapter 14
## The Book of Albert

**Chapter 1: The First Commandment**

1 *T*he mistakes of others serve as beacons to the purity of a successful plan. [2]Preparation, after all, is the first commandment. [3]To plan gives options, options provide flexibility. [4]Immerse yourself in the quiet still of the cool waters and contemplate, my disciple. [5]Reflect and breathe and seek to study the path of others and learn their mistakes and victories. [6]We are all connected in this way, like the Zulu warrior who eats the heart of his conquests, consume the flesh of those who have gone before. [7]Use them like the Hopi tribe used all the parts of the buffalo. [8]So it shall come to pass; so it shall be.

**Chapter 2: The Three Queries**

[1]Consider the three queries. [2]As Socrates admonished us at Delphi, know thyself above all else. [3]Reflect in the darkness of the starry night and stare into the flames and contemplate the answers before proceeding on the path. [4]The greatest focus is this: be centered on the objective. [5]The three queries serve as a

crucible to burn away the superfluous, to bring focus like the mantra of the Om mani padme hum.

[6]The first query: Are those who will die known to you? [7]Revenge and vengeance are reasonable motivations for killing, yet they complicate. [8]Like a laser, focus your goal. [9]Are there certain people who must die to be punished? [10]Must they suffer? [11]If this is your resolution, make this your design. [12]The desire of your heart can be hard like the rocks of the greatest mountain or soft like the lush meadows. [13]The target of your assault should be like these lush meadows of the Psalms. [14]When the heart is hardened and the grievance is fierce, focus is lost. [15]Strike adjacent to the object of your scorn and leave the pain that lasts for an eternity.

[16]The second query: How many will die? [17]For many, the crusade becomes about the artfulness of it. [18]If those who will perish are not known to you, then your strategy will reflect this. [19]Overall, there is no right answer, but rather a question of quality over quantity.

[20]The third query: Must you live? [21]Will you plunge into the abyss with your victims or will you live to see another day in freedom? [22]This is not a question of chance, but rather of focus. [23]This is not a fact, but it is a truth.

**Chapter 3: Cover Your Path**
[1]Be wary of the tracks you leave as you plan. [2]Striking at your heart's desire leads to carelessness. [3]Your own life and freedom can become forfeit and the plan may be ill-conceived. [4]Choose wisely your path; be sly and clever, like the fox. [5]Hunt, and forsake the howl.

[6]Be silent as you cross to your prey, leaving no marks that can be followed. [7]Make your purchases carefully and without credit cards that can be tracked, and remove the sim card from your phone.

[8]Stay hidden and camouflaged as you stalk your prey. [9]Avoid places where you can be observed and when you must be observed, make sure you use a mask, gloves, and camouflage to hide your identity, fingerprints, and DNA.

[10]Do not bark loudly, amplifying your movements through social media. [11]Be focused on your mission and do not telegraph your movements or gloat in your success.

## Chapter 4: The Hammer in Your Hand

[1]I shall be the hammer in your hand, the bullet in your brain. [2]Choose carefully the weapon, the method of destruction. [3]Many choose the wide path of the fancy, sleek, and complicated. [4]Avoid these complications and stay focused on the task at hand. [5]The most efficient killing machine is the bolt of the cattle gun. [6]Metal against bone and flesh.

[7]The pale Galilean, the prophet carpenter, had many hands and many tools. [8]Be prepared when your hammer slips and fails you. [9]Have many tools and many hands; these are the best of plans.

## Chapter 5: The Second Commandment

[1]If the first commandment is preparation, the second commandment is rehearsal. [2]Practice begets perfection. [3]The spider's web is created over time and is a result of practice. [4]Think of your goals and let them wander your mind. [5]Check the bolts securing the grand Ferris wheel to the earth, as once the spinning starts, an ounce of prevention is worth a pound of cure.

[6]When the winds come, the spider has tied its web tightly to the reeds.

[7]When the rain falls, the spider has built a web that reflects the drops of water.

[8]When the locusts prey, the spider loses the web but keeps the feast.

[9]When the fire burns, the spider forgoes its master work to create another day.

[10]Be like the spider, my children. [11]Prepare and rehearse. [12]Be meticulous as thy God who has set the path before you. [13]Travel in my footprints on the beach; I shall carry you and you will never be forsaken.

## Chapter 6: Those Who Stand in Opposition

[1]There are those who stand in opposition to your task. [2]The peacemakers, the gunslingers. [3]Know their processes and their procedures; know them like you know yourself. [4]Their secret folly is in their preparation and methods. [5]They play a game of checkers, methodical and unswerving, leaning into that strength. [6]This is their strength and their weakness. [7]Burn this into your mind: for every Achilles, there is a heel.

[8]Be clever and quiet, my children, deep in the belly of that wooden horse. [9]Play chess to their checkers, be Ulysses to their Achilles.

[10]Anticipate their reaction and guide their hand. [11]As in Aikido, use their force against them and guide them gently to the floor; then have your way with their women, feast on their meat, and plunder their treasures.

## Chapter 7: The Third Commandment

[1]Water has many ways of being; resonating within itself. [2]Each state contradicts the state before it, moving and hiding, like a clear ghost with transparent desires. [3]Be this substance, my children, in all its forms. [4]Hold steady to your ideals and be willing to adjust. [5]Move quickly when the time calls and be patient in the blind, enduring and waiting to strike your prey.

[6]Be like water; hard as ice and focused on your plan.

⁷Be like water; fluid and liquid, adapting to your surroundings.

⁸Be like water; gaseous like steam, hidden yet ever present.

⁹Allow for innovation, as the universe is vast and complex.

**Chapter 8: Afterword**

¹I leave you, my dear children, the followers of my book, with these commandments and teachings. ²Broken free from the stone tablet and existing in hexadecimal and the burning bush of binary LED light. ³I write this for you, take of my body and eat. ⁴Be nourished as you read my words and follow my path, my way.

⁵Take my words and fish. ⁵Be my disciples and take what providence has given you dominion over in all the land, the sea, and sky. ⁶Go forth and multiply, and make me proud.

⁷Leave the sharks to eat their dead.

# Chapter 15
## New Orleans, Spring, Tuesday, 9:45ᵖᵐ

Wagner walked quickly away from Jade and her Tarot cards and covered several blocks before his heart stopped racing. He turned the corner on Chartres and Magnolia and walked down the block to the faded green door with the gate leading to his apartment. He walked through and closed the wrought iron behind him. He took some solace in the old stories that iron kept ghosts and spirits from entering a house.

He thought back to when he first moved to New Orleans. Many of the apartment and real estate postings were listed as haunted or not haunted. He joked with Mauve, his real estate broker, when he first saw this. She had quickly corrected him.

"Oh no, that ain't no joke." She turned her massive frame around in the office chair and came close to him. He could still smell her perfume, something too rich and overpowering. She wore a bright yellow dress that was two sizes too big and seemed to clash with her dark skin. She had been born and raised in Louisiana and had the thick accent that mesmerized Wagner every time he heard it. It reminded him of James Carville, the Ragin' Cajun from LSU.

"People here take their ghosts real serious-like. You're all but required to list the supernatural status of all apartments near and about the Quarter. Down right obligated, I'd say. My sweet Jesus." She crossed herself and seemed to say a quick prayer at all this talk of ghosts.

Wagner climbed the stairs to his third-floor apartment and unlocked the door. As usual, Faulkner bounded up to him. This cat hadn't quite gotten the message about not being a dog. He circled Wagner's leg and purred loudly. "Just happy to see me, eh Faulk?" This cat gave it away. Nothing coy about him.

Wagner rifled through the kitchen and cursed his lack of foresight at neglecting to stock even the most basic of groceries. In a city known for its food, there was just too much temptation to wander down the street to the Grille or Central Grocery to buy a sandwich instead of cooking at home. He had stocked his kitchen a few times, but after throwing out spoiled milk, brown lettuce, and squishy grapes, he realized that there were better ways to spend his money.

Dumb cat, Wagner said to himself. Little fur ball. Wagner pushed past his collection of mixers, tonic, and assorted limes in the refrigerator and found a half-consumed can of cat food wrapped in plastic. He pulled off the cellophane and put the can on the floor. Faulk wasted no time digging in, accompanied with a low, almost growl-like, purr. The can of food slid across the floor as the exuberant and perpetually-hungry cat ate his dinner. Faulkner looked up at him halfway through his can of Fancy Feast and purred contentedly.

The apartment was a small one, much smaller than the house Wagner once lived in. Location trumped floor space here in the Crescent City. He would have opted for an apartment half this size if the location was as good. It was within wandering distance to the House of Blues, One Eyed Jack's, and the assorted music venues of Frenchman Street. Wagner wouldn't have chosen to live anywhere else on the planet. This was his home.

The kitchen was simple, the dishes stacked on open shelves. Asian-style deep bowls and a collection of barware glasses that Wagner had for everyday use. There were a few bottles of liquor lined up against the tiled backsplash next to the sink. Johnny Walker Black, Jameson, and a half-empty bottle of Johnny Walker Blue that Kate, his publisher from Harper, had sent him when he first moved down to celebrate the success of his novel.

Aside from that, the counters were mostly bare, but for the French press he had gotten from his friends when he moved. Of course, he rarely made coffee at home and opted for one of the dozen coffee shops sprinkled throughout the city. PJ's was a favorite, with its deep-set leather chairs and ideal people-watching location by the intersection of Chartres and St. Peter by Jackson Square.

His eye caught on the bowl that Jackie had gotten for him the third or fourth night that she had stayed over. It was faded ceramic with a dog painted on it. An excited cartoon dog looking very happy to be fed. It had a little rubber mat attached to the bottom to keep it from sliding on the kitchen floor. She had gotten this for Faulkner. She would make this face when he ate, growling and purring and pushing the tin across the floor. This thought made Wagner sad, though he wasn't sure why.

He clicked the light in the bedroom and kicked off his boots. He usually carried a small messenger bag with him that held a notebook or laptop to use if the mood to write struck him. It had been a few years since his last book. Despite the initial high sales, the royalty checks had started to diminish while the phone calls for another manuscript had increased. It wasn't quite writer's block, nothing so mundane. That problem never troubled Wagner. It was something different. Like he was relegated to sketches that never really added up to something significant. Something meaningful.

The bed was an unmade mess, as usual, as he liked it. Too many pillows scattered amongst soft sheets and a tangle of blankets. A ceiling fan spun in its lazy, continuous cycle above him. The rest of the room was sparse, with a bedside table made from upcycled wood and a closet mostly filled with clothes he never wore. An assortment of t-shirts and jeans were slung over the leather chair in the corner. Wagner had gotten the chair at an estate sale a few months ago. He never sat in it but liked the way it looked in the corner.

He went back into the kitchen/living room and lit a few of the candles in the old non-working fireplace in the corner. The brick walls and fireplace had been a selling point for the apartment, that and the hardwood floors. Mauve warned him about the fireplace not working. "That there isn't gonna work and won't never work. So, you can't have fires here. Not that you should have fires anywhere in the city. We had enough of that in 1788. My Jesus, this whole city. Either burning up or underwater. My sweet Jesus."

He knew she wouldn't have liked the candles. They were perfectly safe on the brick and with all of their use had accumulated a rather nice collection of white wax shaped into a landscape across the hearth. Wagner liked the candlelight and did most of his writing in the deep leather chair that sat next to the fireplace.

The chair had been a spree purchase, and he had a hell of a time working with the movers to get it up the steps. It was wide and took effort to climb in and out of. It had come from the high-end, sophisticated, vintage-style store Restored Antiques. A Churchill, he thought. That's what it was called. Either that or Churchill was the name of the leather color. He couldn't remember. He had a love/hate relationship with places like that. It was a nice chair, but they sold him a story. Like the narrator in *Fight Club*, "What kind of dining set defines me as a person?"

Wagner didn't have a TV. He wasn't necessarily against television, but there was something about it that depressed him. Watching other people do things. He had never really followed sports and the news didn't interest him. If he wanted to watch something, he would pull it up online. There was more there than he could possibly watch anyway. That and Wagner was a more of a movie buff. He had several of his favorites saved as files on the bottom of his desktop. An eclectic mix: *Breakfast at Tiffany's, Casablanca, The Matrix, Fight Club, The Big Lebowski, Barfly, Groundhog Day, Apocalypse Now*. He liked his movies to match his mood. In some ways, the files were like old friends he would invite over when he was feeling down. They picked him up and walked him safely across his darker, broodier times. Another occupational hazard for a writer, he supposed.

The apartment's main decorations were books. They rested in a haphazard fashion throughout. Wagner had two long and deep wooden bookshelves that held a dozen or so volumes on each shelf. These were packed full in a way that would have made sense to a hoarder. After all of the proper space was taken up, books fought for position in a precarious balancing act. Hemingway, Fitzpatrick, Gaiman, Bukowski, and Thompson filled the shelves. He had a few from Agatha Christie's Hercule Poirot phase and some Flannery O'Connor. Writer's books. Inspiration. Gaiman was his favorite, the story of Door and Richard Mahew in London Below. Several piles of brown moleskin notebooks sat on one shelf containing writing sketches and ideas for future stories.

He fell onto the chair and stretched his legs out on the ottoman. It was early still, not yet 10, and Wagner thought about writing some. He certainly had experienced enough thought-provoking occurrences tonight to feel inspired. Yet, that was the problem; they never really quite tied together into something larger. Something with meaning. Not that the first book had any meaning. Not really. But that was different; that one he wrote for the money. After writing that way, he wasn't sure there was anything left. He sold part of himself writing that. However, if you are going to sell out, at least make some good money when they take your soul.

He thought about the cups, running in his mind all in a row. It was strange that the cards fell like that for him. More than strange, really. It reminded him of the classic scene from Disney's *Fantasia*. The brooms lining up and carrying an infinite number of buckets of water. That poor mouse fighting against the inevitable tide. That movie always gave Wagner the chills. It was this dark feeling of being out of control and afraid. It made him feel sad and scared all at once. Like something had been started and he didn't have control over it any longer. He pitied Mickey in that movie. It made him anxious to watch.

He took his small laptop from where it was wedged between the cushion and the side of the chair. The screen flickered on and Faulkner, long since done with his meal, took up his position at Wagner's feet. Wagner stretched out in the chair and considered the day. He opened his computer and began to jot down some of the events. His eyes felt heavy. Wagner found himself losing the battle to stay awake. And why fight it? He didn't have anywhere to be in the morning. Not anymore. He could catch up some tomorrow with the writing. Maybe call Kate later in the day and make up some kind of story about his next project. Maybe that would buy him a few weeks. But now, a little nap; just for a moment.

He was in London, under Queen Mary's bridge by the Eye of London. The tunnel was cold, but tolerable. Centuries-old brick was darkened by the smoke of countless fires to keep the cold at bay. Wagner looked to the end of the bridge and away from the man.

An old man was pressed against the stone. He wore a tattered khaki coat with a dirty black t-shirt. He held a light brown notebook in his lap and he wrote carefully, lifting his head occasionally in thought. He had two signs on either side of a red and black hat with some coins and some crumpled bills inside it. One sign read, "Anything is a blessing" while the other was written in shaky black marker with the words, "Embarrassed. Hungry." There was a backpack next to him with writing and symbols on it.

Wagner walked by him, saying nothing. He wasn't sure why he was in London. He had been a few times but it had been years since he was last there. Of course, London held a special place in his mind, given Gaiman's book, London above and London Below.

Wagner paused crossing the tunnel and turned back, trying to make out the man's face in the poor light. He leaned closer and tried to get a better look. The more he leaned in, the harder it was to see. It was as if the light was working against him in some kind of illusion. The man wrote and the shadows became darker. And when he was close, so very close, then he saw his own face, his own eyes looking back at him. Cold and in pain.

Wagner woke with a start. Faulkner did not care for this and looked at Wagner sleepily.

The dream reminded Wagner of a recurrent nightmare he used to have in childhood. He was alone in his house and heard someone cooking in the kitchen. Banging pots around and humming to himself. Wagner walked down the hall in slow motion. Closer and closer; past the beige phone hanging on the wall and the side of the refrigerator with the erasable pen and the smudged whiteboard. Past the wooden desk on the left where his father paid the bills. He turned and saw a figure to the right, in front of the stove. The figure turned, and his face was Wagner's face, smiling back at him with a too-wide Cheshire cat grin. The smile grew and grew until it was unbelievably big; too big for his face. And then it would take the iron pan it was cooking with, this bizzaro-Wagner, and swing it in a wide arc, grease spraying around the kitchen and whatever meat had been cooking flying against the wall into the clock. And then Wagner just heard the sound. The sound of a loud cartoon gong right as the frying pan slammed into his head.

He set the laptop down and sat up in his chair and stretched. The clock read 11pm. He realized he was very, very hungry. He hadn't eaten all day, distracted by drinking, strip clubs, and music. His stomach protested at this idea of not having food in it. He stood up and stretched more fully. He went to the bathroom and straightened his mop of hair in the mirror, relieved himself, and then headed toward the door, grabbing his boots from the bedroom. He thought about laying back down on the den of pillows and blankets. It was late, but he knew a place. He always knew somewhere to go.

The Crescent City Grille wasn't reviewed favorably if one looked it up online or sought a recommendation from the hotel concierge. It was a 24-hour dive diner at the far end of Dauphine Street, which ran parallel to Bourbon. It was well known by locals as something of a late-night oasis for those lucky few who wandered by in the early hours of the morning after a night of drinking.

It was only a short walk from Wagner's apartment. The streets were quiet, although there were still some folks wandering about, working through their late-night drinking, spilling what remained in their plastic green hand-grenade cups onto the street while beads bounced wildly around their necks.

"Shit," Wagner said. "Jackie."

He took out his phone and texted her, hoping that she hadn't already left for the night. He typed, "Hey, sorry. Fell asleep. Meet me at the Grille for a burger?" He hit send and was pissed at himself for forgetting. Maybe he was the problem with them. He was just so flighty, couldn't keep plans. They had that fight before.

Wagner walked on in the night. A third-floor balcony had a light on in the window and a ceiling fan that cast repetitive light and shadow patterns across the wall and plants. Wagner watched the fan for a moment as he walked down the street.

The Grille just had a few people occupying its narrow footprint. The counter sat about ten; three or four of those seats were filled with people staring at the grill. The short-order cook juggled several orders of burgers and tater tots beneath the large silver hubcaps that kept the grease and steam all contained as the meat sizzled and cooked. He checked his phone. No answer from Jackie.

A thin black man in an ill-fitting apron was at the register on the right-hand side of the bar. He had several hand-tied necklaces hanging around his neck and several colored wristbands announcing various charities and fun walks he had participated in. This was Daryl, the night manager.

Wagner watched as Daryl had an argument with a homeless man who was attempting to cash in his panhandling change for dollar bills. Wagner imagined the liquor store frowned on pennies and nickels when trying to buy a bottle of cheap bourbon.

The homeless man had a thick and unkempt beard and a thin face. He wore a tattered green army jacket and small wool cap. He already had a crumpled paper bag wrapped around a glass bottle. Maddog or some other kind of fortified wine, Wagner imagined. He had a faded and dirty coffee cup in his other hand. He used this to collect the spare coins tossed at him throughout the day. The edges were worn from where his fingers had rubbed the Styrofoam thin.

"Now listen," Daryl said, "I ain't got time for this. I already told you that you gave me change for seven dollars, not nine. I just counted it out in front of you! I'm not going to do it again." Daryl nodded at Wagner when he came in and said, "Hey there, Wags. Bar okay?"

Wagner nodded and took a seat a few down from the register, away from Daryl, who continued to argue with the homeless man.

Across the restaurant, a balding man in a faded orange polo shirt and jeans was about halfway through a cheeseburger and fries. Four tourists from Japan sat talking quickly and smiling often over hamburgers and tater tots. Maps of the city were scattered across the table. The two women in the party had their phones out and were texting, thumbs moving quickly across the screens.

Wagner was two seats down from a big man in a tight fitting t-shirt. He wore red sweatpants with black Velcro strap sneakers and rocked back and forth on his stool. Wagner assumed he had some kind of mental health problem. He was eating a piece of pie and quietly talking to himself.

"Fine! Just fine. Here. Nine dollars. Here." Daryl slammed down a five and four singles. "Now get out. I have people waiting and we ain't no bank here."

The homeless man in the ripped t-shirt took the money and mumbled something like, "it was my money anyway..." and wandered out into the night.

Wagner took two dollars out of his pocket and slid them over to Daryl and said, "Sorry about that drama, man. They turning you into a bank out here in the badlands?"

Daryl pocketed the two dollars and thanked Wagner. "You have no idea, my friend. No idea. What'll it be?"

Wagner ordered a burger and tots, a specialty of the house. He added an Abita beer to the order and sat back to wait.

Daryl went over to the big man in the t-shirt and red sweatpants and asked if he needed anything. The man reminded Wagner of Lennie from *Of Mice and Men*. Huge and lumbering, but a bit of a gentle giant. He nodded back at Daryl enthusiastically as he chewed his pie. "Some milk." Pause. Chew, chew, chew. "Please." Daryl smiled at Lennie and brought him a glass of milk to go with his pie. Well, not a glass, but rather a chipped plastic Coca-Cola cup half filled with milk.

The Japanese tourists were ready to check out. The two men came up and attempted to pay for their meal. They held the check and asked in broken English to have it separated so they could pay individually. Daryl looked annoyed at this and shook his head vehemently even before they could finish their question. While saying "No, no, no...," he rummaged for a torn paper copy of the menu. He pointed out the text at the bottom that said in bold print "NO SEPARATE CHECKS." The tourists looked at each other puzzled.

The menu of the Crescent City Grille was a poorly printed, photocopied mess that changed color from week to week, despite the fact that the food choices changed very little. Wagner suspected it was Ken, the owner of the Grille, constantly tinkering with the rules for appropriate behavior. Among Wagner's favorites were, "Have character... don't be one," "Everyone brings happiness into this business... some when they come in, others when they leave," and "No talking to yourself. Keep both hands on the table."

This amused Wagner at first. He thought it was a tongue-in-cheek attempt at quirkiness and humor. After he spent more than a few nights having a burger at the Grille, he learned the last two sentences were actually a set of needed rules. He had watched Daryl scold several people for touching themselves under the table, and people talking loudly to themselves was a common occurrence.

This last part made Wager think of the woman with the baloney in her mouth talking to herself and then yelling at him. What had she said? Something about being empty and that no one would die for him. That last part sounded familiar, but he couldn't place the words.

The tourists relented and paid their bill together by pooling their money. Wagner fumbled through this week's salmon-colored menu and laughed at a new addition to the rules. Underneath the section of the menu that reviewed the side order options, they had added, "We don't eat in your bed, so please don't sleep at our table. You've paid the price, now look at how much you have gained."

Wagner pondered that last part. It made sense to add a rule about not sleeping, as this was a constant battle he had seen the staff fight with customers. He wasn't sure what the other part meant. Like you paid for your food and you should look around? Or was it some reference to a Bible verse? Jesus paid the price for all of us sinners down here so we could gain the kingdom of heaven? Either way it was strange, even for Ken.

There was a bell. Daryl reached around and brought Wagner's burger and tots from the side of the grill and sat them in front of him.

Wagner gestured to the new text at the bottom of the menu. "Daryl, what's this part about what you've gained?"

He shrugged and said, "Man, I have no idea. You know Ken, he's always messing with that damn menu." Daryl went back to going through the night's receipts and balancing the cash register.

Wagner ate his burger quickly, occasionally pausing to dip a tot in the pool of ketchup sprinkled liberally with salt that occupied the left-hand side of his plate. Two attractive young women came in, one blonde and one brunette. They laughed and joked with each other in a loud and drunk kind of way. They asked Daryl where they should sit.

"Anywhere you want, ladies. You take a load off your feet," Daryl responded.

They took seats at the table across from the balding man with the orange polo and went back to discussing the events from their night.

Wagner looked up and felt the hairs on the back of his neck as they stood at attention. He had this surreal feeling. He thought of the man who sat in the foreground of Edward Hopper's

*Nighthawks.* He felt like that. With his back to the world, to all the people who walked by and looked at him. Wagner turned slowly and had this eerie feeling like from his nightmare. He expected to see himself with that wide smile and frying pan waiting for him as he turned.

Then he saw her. The girl. She walked by the glass window and her dog trotted beside her. Like a vision from some kind of post-apocalyptic movie, she was still dressed in earth tones and her hair was a combination of dreadlocks and blonde dust.

She caught Wagner's eye and smiled at him again; that challenging smile. She passed down the street.

Wagner wasn't hungry anymore. He paid for his half-eaten meal and was out the door into the night after her.

She was up ahead of him and turned down St. Phillip Street. Wagner followed her down and saw her pause at the opening to a building he hadn't seen before. Not uncommon in the city. It had this way of shifting and changing, even for locals. Twin gas lamps stood outside of the entryway and she disappeared between them.

Wagner quickened his pace and caught up to where she had gone. He stood in front of the gas lamps that flickered in the darkness. The lettering on the sign was faded. Wagner made out La Chute. An odd name; French clearly, but he had no idea what it meant.

There was a lengthy passageway, about the width of a man's shoulders, that opened forward in front of him. Wagner wasn't surprised to discover a new place after coming to this part of New Orleans for years. The city was like that. Many of the restaurants and bars had closed and would reopen under new management with new names.

He couldn't see much in the passage in front of him. Wagner walked down cautiously as his eyes adjusted to the darkness. As he walked, he began to make out a sizeable and foreboding wooden door with a massive iron handle. There was no sign of the girl and the dog. There was no light here. He looked back and saw the shadows of the flickering gas lamps.

He opened the door and went inside.

# Chapter 16
## New Orleans, Spring, Tuesday, 9:45ᵖᵐ

"In a moment of final, blinding rage, Cora pushed her sister as she stood on the balcony looking out into the night. Madeline fell into the darkness. This is where she died."

Ella took a deep drink from the beer, feeling the length of the day on her. Well, that and the warmth Coop had left with her. Mostly, she just wanted to be done and be asleep, but she also had this excitement at seeing him play tonight. She loved watching him perform. Just another hour and she'd be able to see him. She went on with the story.

"Cora was caught and convicted for her crime. The penalty for murder, even accidental, was quite severe. She was confined to prison for the rest of her natural life. As for Mr. Locke? He was quite devastated. He traveled far away from his home town of New Orleans. He lost himself in his merchant ships and business. He hoped he could hide from his one true love, but a man cannot hide from his thoughts, can he? Mr. Locke never married, nor did he ever return to New Orleans." Ella finished and surveyed her tour group.

The tour was large tonight, about 30, and Dave had said his group was about the same. This happened sometimes, just these large bookings at random times. Eh, the more the merrier. The woman who had the cannonball shots was there. She was tall and thin, and held an old, brown, long-haired Chihuahua in her arms. She had the dog wrapped up in a pink and black blanket. Ella thought maybe he needed it, because he was shivering something fierce. The dog growled at the two black men standing closest to her. The woman pulled him close within the blanket and said, "Aw, you stop that now," in a vaguely condescending and reproachful way. The dog snuggled deeper into the blanket and regarded the men with caution. Upon closer observation, it was apparent that most of the woman's teeth were missing and she had a poorly done script neck tattoo that was faded and difficult to read. Ella figured meth was the culprit here.

In the distance, there was the sound of a muffled thud. Like a car backfiring somewhere near Canal Street.

The woman then addressed the black men, "See, he don't mind you." And then to her dog, "Don't know why you're growling. They're the same." She looked for support from a young, blonde woman wearing a green Jansport backpack who stood next to her. She had sad eyes, like she had reached for help too many times and always came up empty. Her hair came down in tangles, and she wore an oversized sweater that hid her frame. Most people would have found the cable-knit sweater too warm, even on a night tour, but she seemed to disappear into its safety, like a turtle in a shell. She successfully avoided the meth lady's eyes and watched Ella, waiting for the story to continue.

Ella found the comment racist, like the tall woman was clarifying this out loud to express that she hadn't raised a racist dog. Which for Ella, made it seem like she had, in fact, raised a racist dog.

"On nights like tonight, while walking the streets of the Quarter, Madeline's ghost can still be seen. She wears a white dress and a wedding veil. If you listen carefully, over the din of the jazz music and the ruckus from Bourbon, she can be heard calling to Mr. Locke.

"…my dear love, Mr. Locke. My dear, dear love…"

"Oh! I very much liked that story!" said an older woman with a red sweater and black pants who then began to cough very loudly. It was that kind of deep chest cough that was either an early stage of bronchitis or pneumonia. Ella was sure it would have scared the country doctor in the early 19th century, but apparently it was not as debilitating as it once was. 'Cause here she was on her tour.

She stood next to two other older women who wore shapeless dresses to allow for maximum movement in the heat. They reminded Ella of the Yep-Yep, Nope-Nope Martians on *Sesame Street*. The coughing woman was a large lady, but not enormous. She had on homemade jewelry, round aqua stones with gold circles closing in on themselves in a kind of fractal design. Faint sounds of sirens came from the top of Bourbon Street near Canal.

"Would you like some gum?" one of the women in the shapeless dresses asked her. "I don't have any cough drops, I'm afraid. But I have some gum."

The woman stopped coughing long enough to take the gum from them. She scratched at the back of her head with intensity as she searched for some kind of relief that never came. Her breathing was labored from the coughing. She inhaled deeply, as if never quite getting enough oxygen. She apologized to the two elderly women next to her and clasped her hands together in an odd gesture, with her fingers outstretched. She said, "I hate those people who cough all the way through the show or a tour. I usually remember to bring cough drops, but I didn't this time. And I feel just terrible."

A middle-aged couple watched this exchange. The man gave an exasperated look to his wife, who was dressed in jeans and a New Orleans School of Cooking sweatshirt. She held her little ghost fan in her hand and waved it absentmindedly at her face. He wore a Git-R-Done hat with a playboy bunny on the top of it, just in case anyone had any lingering confusion on the double entendre. His t-shirt had a stick figure on its hands and knees and the words, "My Indian name is Crawling Drunk." He brought a mostly empty bag of Zapp's Cajun Crawtator chips to his mouth and shook the crumbs into it.

Sigh. Ella thought about how many groups you could offend at once with just an outfit. She decided it was better to get them walking again. She led them toward the old section of fence with the padlocks, next to Barracks and Chartres.

An old homeless man was nestled against some green porch steps. He looked up from his intense scribbling in a light brown notebook as they came closer. Ella read his first cardboard sign. It was written in shaky black marker, "Anything is a blessing" and then "Embarrassed. Hungry" on the second as she passed him. There was another muffled thud in the distance, this time from the Mississippi side behind her. Perhaps another backfire. But Ella wondered; it didn't sound like a backfire.

"Hey," someone in the tour group said to the Yep-Yep ladies. "Hey, I smoke cigarettes. It's a bad habit, but you know. Do you have any?"

The voice was slurred and the women didn't respond. The guy stumbled. His friend held him up. It had been a long day in the city.

"Billy!" his friend said. He had been drinking as well, but he wasn't drunk. Not yet. "Billy, you sound like a crazy person asking for a cigarette that way out here."

A younger woman in glasses pushed past Billy with a loud "Excuse me!" Her glasses were too big for her face and they made her look much older than she was. Billy stumbled again, and her hand brushed up against his mostly white t-shirt with some kind of mustard colored stain on the bottom corner.

Excuse Me Lady was followed by a short man who carried a number of shopping bags with him from their day's adventures. She made a huffing noise after brushing Billy's shirt and asked her companion with the bags for the Purell. He juggled the bags and reached into his pocket to produce a small bottle of hand sanitizer. She gave Billy and his friend a dirty look, spread the clear goo on her hands, and wiped them vigorously together. As they dried she reached into her windbreaker jacket pocket and took out a small lotion that she rubbed angrily on her hands before returning it to its home in her pocket. She mumbled something Ella couldn't quite hear to the man holding the bags about the city's humidity.

Ella was trying to keep the tour group moving. The friend was doing his best to hold Billy up, but he was fighting a losing battle. Billy focused on his feet, somewhat amazed they would hold him up.

"I just need a smoke," Billy said.

"I know, but when you ask like that you sound like a crazy homeless person wandering in the Quarter," the friend replied and dragged him forward so they didn't lose the tour group.

As luck would have it, the pair caught the attention of a tall, lanky man wearing ill-fitting sweatpants and a Pelican's t-shirt. The man looked at the pair and said, "What the actual fuck did you say?!?"

Billy's friend went into overdrive. "Oh no, man. I wasn't talking to you." Billy looked around confused, the nuances of the miscommunication clearly lost on him.

"I'm not homeless," Sweatpants said, raising his voice. "I have a home right over there at Covenant House."

"Come on group, keep up," Ella said and pulled her mob through the streets of the city.

A brunette with curly, dark hair, a blue shirt, and a short, pink-flower skirt touched Ella on her shoulder. She was accompanied by a tall man with a full, thick beard, a pastel colored striped tank top, and hat with white lettering that read "Pelican Cove." A large pelican seemed to be holding a hurricane drink. The tall man had a Peg-Leg Pete's go-cup in his hand.

He said to Ella, "We heard there was a slave house around here that was on the TV show with the witches? American Horror?" And before she could answer, the woman said, "Oh yes! And I have to say I just love your outfit. This tour is amazing. I love Anne Rice. Didn't she live somewhere here in the quarter?"

"Yeah, we heard that too, but then she or Nicolas Cage sold their…"

Ella stopped listening and watched the woman. She thought she was the kind of woman who could have been quite beautiful if you looked at her in just the right way. She brought out a ChapStick from a small pocket on her skirt and coated her lips. She brought the bottom lip over the top and then the top over the bottom. And then the ChapStick disappeared. This left Ella with a kind of in-between feeling of vague sexuality and meticulous action that never quite came together. More sirens in the distance now, both uptown toward Bourbon and toward the river. Never a dull moment in this city.

The group followed her and she pointed out interesting facts about the Quarter and the fire of 1788. She brought them to the fence and said, "These are offerings people leave for Madeline and her dearest, Mr. Locke. You may return to pay your respects, if you wish. It's always best to keep the ghosts happy in our city."

She saw Dave's group up ahead and looked at her watch, a little after 10. She was running late. They took up most of the street corner by Dauphine. Back to the Marigny for her second tale of the night. She greeted Dave with a warm hug as the groups came together.

A group of three people stood leaning against the wall as Ella and Dave caught up with each other. There was an athletic black man in a form-fitting t-shirt and silver chain with a cross around his neck. He had his arm around a fit blonde who had short-cropped hair. She had a contagious, happy smile. Next to them stood a younger woman with dark hair tied into pigtails.

Ella asked Dave about the thuds in the distance and the sirens. He had heard them as well but didn't have any ideas what they could be. They shrugged it off and Dave gave her an encouraging "Go get 'em!" Ella stood under the flickering gas lamp to tell her tale.

"You see, Captain Malick was not quite a pirate, there was no Jolly Roger on his ship's mast. But he was a thief, nonetheless, and he would take from those he came across. Most thought the true valuables were in the cargo hold, or in the Captain's stateroom, but Malick had his eye on something else."

The group had merged, a crowd of close to sixty people with little ghost fans and many with drinks in their hands. There were fewer children on the late tour, though there were a few hanging onto the day as they watched Ella pace back and forth in front of them, her pale skin shining in the light of the gas lamp.

A nervous mother fretted over her four-year-old. He was too old for his stroller and a bit too young to be hearing the story of Captain Malick cannibalizing his victims. Her husband was arguing with their teenage daughter, who was texting on her phone instead of listening to the story. Ella wanted to point out that the arguing was more disruptive than the texting, but she let it go.

"You see, Malick didn't just want grain and blankets and fine furs and rifles; which might be what you would think he would want, if you were on a merchant ship being boarded. But not Malick. He wanted something from each ship he stopped. Something more..."

Ella paused to say, "more personal." That was the next line in the story. But then a red dot appeared on Billy's white shirt, about a foot from the mustard stain at the bottom. It was small at first and then spread like a starfish unfurling when returned to the ocean. Billy looked down in drunken amazement.

She saw a bright light in the darkness behind the tour group. And then more, coming in short bursts.

FLASH FLASH FLASH
POP POP POP
FLASH FLASH FLASH
POP POP POP

There was a slight delay between the flash and the gunshot. Ella remembered something about this in Mrs. Humphrey's 9th grade science class. Light and sound traveled at different velocities. The Dobber effect? Was that it?

She saw the young blonde woman with the Jansport backpack. Her sweater was stained with blood and the left side of her face was missing. Ella was frozen. More gunshots echoed in the night.

POP POP POP
POP POP POP
POP POP POP

One of the *Sesame Street* Martian women, Yep-Yep, screamed and pulled her friend to the ground. There was a growing red stain near the upper part of the dress. Nope-Nope tried to get up and was hit by gunfire and fell back to the ground.

POP POP POP
POP POP POP
POP POP POP

Ella clamped her hands over her ears and thought, that wasn't it. That was the house elf in Harry Potter. Dobby. It was the Doppler Effect. Dave grabbed her by the arm and tried to pull her down to the street. Zazu exploded in a puff of stuffing. The next round took Dave between the eyes. He slouched forward and lost Ella's arm, an expression of surprise on his face.

The mother screamed as bullets tore through the crowd, hitting the stroller, her toddler, her teenage daughter, and husband. Her daughter's iPhone fell to the ground near Ella and she was surprised that the glass didn't shatter. The mother didn't seem to be hit, but screamed and looked around with wild, animal eyes.

POP POP POP
POP POP POP
POP POP POP

Parts of the group tried to run away down the street. Chips of brick and dust flew off the walls. The athletic black man shoved the blonde to the ground and ran for the nearest parked car across the street. Others started to break away from the group and run.

POP POP POP
POP POP POP
POP POP POP
POP POP POP

The man running towards the nearest car spun when the bullets ripped into him. He fell lifeless to the street. The young woman with the pigtails and beads ran out after him and was gunned down just as quickly.

Then it was quiet. Ella could feel her heart beating in her chest. She thought about the knife on her thigh but couldn't make her hands move. She had this insane thought about bringing a knife to a gunfight. Her mind was struggling to keep up.

Then there was some yelling. Ella saw a dark figure down the street. It was the person who was doing this. He wore a long black cloak and a wolf mask. His hands reached for something under his cloak and he dropped a thin, foot-long rectangular box to the ground. He was the big, bad wolf.

"He's reloading. We can stop him!" This came from Git-R-Done Hat. His wife was breathing quick and shallow and bleeding from dark wounds on her leg and arm. He tossed off his hat and ran at the cloaked figure. Most of the group stayed frozen against the wall or on the ground. The curly-haired woman in the short pink-flower skirt stood shaking on the sidewalk crying hysterically and pointing at the blood-covered tank top of her boyfriend. His Peg-Leg Pete's cup lay on its side, the remainder of the hurricane drink slowly mixing with the blood on the sidewalk.

The wolf let the large object in his hands fall when he saw Git-R-Done running at him looking to relive his football glory days and make one last tackle for his hometown sweetheart. The rifle caught on the tactical strap and hung to the left under the cloak. The wolf drew the Glock and took a moment to aim. Then he fired three shots in rapid succession. The first missed the charging man, but hit the fretting mother and wife screaming wildly in the dark as she went down.

The next bullet hit Git-R-Done in the chest. He stopped running and looked surprised. The next found a home in his chest across the printed slur. He went down for good.

The wolf holstered the Glock and took another rectangular box from inside the cape. The rifle was in his hands again and the plastic clip was slapped into place as he drew back the bolt. There were maybe a half dozen people left, mostly huddled against the wall in front of Ella. He fired into this group as he walked forward.

FLASH FLASH FLASH
POP POP POP
FLASH FLASH FLASH
POP POP POP
FLASH FLASH FLASH
POP POP POP

It was hard for Ella to take her eyes away from the muzzle. The flashes and rifle bursts melted into one. The glass surrounding the torch shattered and the flame went out. The huddled group stopped moving. In the distance, she could see one or two people running down the street, likely out of range of the gunman. It was dark and the lights from down Dauphine cast a halo around the wolf as he approached. His shadow was long in front of him and it reached for her like a gnarled hand.

Ella heard harsh coughing from behind her as the wolf fired three more shots. She turned to see the woman in the red sweater and black pants fall dead in the street.

The wolf let the rifle hang at his side. She heard in the distance the faint sounds of sirens and hope.

It was quiet again. The gunman took out the pistol and walked through what remained of the crowd. He took aim the heads of anyone who moved or whimpered. Then he shot them still. Each time the gun fired, Ella shuddered and sank lower, until she was laying on the street in the fetal position.

"Well, well." The voice came from above her. "It looks like it's just you and me left." She heard the spent clip falling to the ground and the new clip being smacked into place. The gunman pulled back the action of the pistol and chambered a bullet.

"You know," the wolf said, impossibly close to her, "I don't think little girls should go walking in these spooky old woods alone."

Ella thought of the "Li'l Red Riding Hood" song by Sam the Sham & The Pharaohs.

Officer Chris Thompson from the NOPD came around the corner quickly; gun drawn. He was a three-year vet on the force and was short, compact, and ready for the fight. He saw the cloaked figure with the gun standing above the woman. Before pulling the trigger, he saw the piles of bodies in the street. It looked like a war zone. There were so many bodies.

The wolf didn't hear Thompson come around the corner. The mask, while excellent for intimidating defenseless mobs of people in the middle of listening to a ghost story, had really shit peripheral vision. Thompson unloaded the first three shots low and to the right, chipping up bits of the street.

He over-compensated as the wolf turned toward him and raised the gun. Thompson's next three shots hit to the left on the brick wall. He steadied his aim and two shots hit solid in the gunman's chest. The wolf stumbled back and the officer fired two more. One clipped the wolf in the shoulder and the other went high again into the wall. The gunman's pistol fell to the ground.

Thompson quickly reloaded his service weapon and looked around to see if his backup had arrived. Not yet. He had called it in and ran to where the shots were coming from. Active shooter protocol and all, he played it by the book. But the book didn't have anything in it about a goddamn wolf who killed dozens of people. And the book didn't account for the fact that most of the force was already out responding to the explosions on Canal and the riverfront. And then the device found at the St. Louis Cathedral steps. There weren't a lot of free NOPD officers around.

The wolf stood straight with the rifle in his hands. He took aim as the officer fumbled with the clip of his gun. A single shot caught Thompson in the chest. He went down hard and his gun spun off into the darkness.

Both wore tactical vests. But only one of them had used armor piercing rounds in their weapon. This why the wolf picked up his pistol from the street and why Thompson lay on the ground bleeding out.

The wolf turned to Ella. He hummed to himself, "What full lips you have. They're sure to lure someone bad…."

Ella said one word. "Wait."

The wolf pulled the trigger and ended her life.

"Aaah-oooooooooh!" he howled and walked off into the night.

# The Witching Hour

# Chapter 17
# New Orleans, Spring, Wednesday, Midnight

"Welcome, sir!" Wagner was greeted by a well dressed maître d' with an abundance of positive energy and excitement. Wagner felt, well…he thought for a moment; he supposed he felt *expected*.

"Umm, hello," Wagner replied cautiously.

"We have been saving a place for you. Please, come this way," the maître d' intoned happily.

He wore a classic-cut tuxedo and was older than Wagner, perhaps in his early sixties. His hair was grey and cut short and professional. He was not a handsome man, but he certainly looked distinguished and took pride in his work. There was a small white folded handkerchief in his lapel pocket. He regarded Wagner with curious and energetic eyes.

The door opened into a dimly lit vestibule lined with Victorian-style chaise lounges and a wide, ornate dark mahogany cabinet along the far wall. A thin wooden podium stood with a ledger on it with a list of names written in blue ink. The maître d' walked Wagner to the book and picked up a silver and black pen. Wagner recognized the starburst white of the Monte Blanc company. "Mr. Sinclair, I assume?"

"Yes," Wagner said. "Have we met? I don't think I know you."

The maître d' smiled a practiced smile, wide and without any guile or pretense. "We have not had the pleasure yet, sir. But I must admit, I am a fan of your writing. I recognize you from the back cover of your book. I am a great admirer." Wagner offered a polite, "Thank you. It's always a pleasure to meet someone who enjoyed my work." The maître d' uncapped the fountain pen and made a check mark next to the name Wagner Sinclair written halfway down the page. There were a dozen or so names on the page, about half had check marks next to them.

"Right this way, sir."

"May, I ask you something…I'm sorry, I don't know your name." Wagner caught the eye of the maître d'.

"Landen, sir. And yes, it would be my pleasure to assist you," the maître d' replied.

"Landen. Yes. Have you by any chance seen a girl come through? Not, you know, a little girl, but a woman. Around 19 or 20? Blonde hair with some dreadlocks? Earth-tone clothes? She had a brown dog with her. Kind of a cute mutt?"

"Yes, of course. She was here just a moment ago." Landen gestured behind him to the twin staircases that opened on either side of the far wall of the vestibule.

## Wolf Howling

Between the twin staircases circling to the room below, there was a framed oil painting on the wall that drew Wagner's eye. It was the beaches on the shores of Africa. There were tall, thin trees building to forests to the edge of the beach. The sands were white and inviting. Immediately off center to the right of the beach were three lions, laying on the sand.

The most startling part of the picture was how the artist captured the blue-green ocean as the dusk fell over the trees and beach. It was as if they had perfectly captured the concept of dusk, just at that very moment of transition from late afternoon to evening.

"Where do the staircases go?" Wagner asked, following Landen.

"Why…" Landen paused and smiled, "They go down, sir." Landen chuckled to himself. It was a good-natured laugh, and Wagner could tell this was an old and practiced joke that amused the maître d' greatly.

"Forgive me," Landen continued, still regaining his composure. "My poor attempt at humor. The steps lead to the antechamber below. You are expected. Just watch your footing here. The path is not as well-lit as it should be."

Wagner followed Landen down the stairs and realized this whole thing didn't make any sense.

"Tell me, Landen. These steps. This antechamber. I thought New Orleans was too wet and swampy to allow for cellars or basement rooms."

"Things here, sir, are" Landen paused for effect, "different, of course." The steps were carpeted marble, with gold colored rods holding the carpet in place.

"Different? I don't understand."

"You are expected, sir. There is nothing to be concerned about," Landen said and reached a wooden door with an antique brass handle. The maître d' opened the door and waited for Wagner to step through.

"Is there anything else you require, sir?" Landen held the door open and waited for Wagner.

"Aren't you coming in?" Wagner asked.

The maître d' looked surprised. "Why, no, sir. I am not expected."

Wagner passed Landen and noticed something about him that he had not caught before. There was a single round hole beneath the perfectly folded white handkerchief. It was about the size of a penny and was only noticeable up close due to the dark fabric. It stood out because everything else about him was so meticulously well-groomed and professional. It seemed like a careless and odd oversight, for someone who appeared so fastidious.

Wagner entered the antechamber below La Chute. The room was large, but exceedingly dark, only lit by table candles and a few accent lights. The overall effect was ideal for the space and Wagner felt as if this was, in many ways, the most perfect room he had ever been in.

Exposed beams of wood crossed the ceiling and were set against copper accents and cast-iron lashings and fasteners. The floor was made from a smooth antique wood and covered by a crisscrossed collection of intricately woven Persian and Indian carpets. Tables with comfortable leather chairs were set back into the far corners of the room and were lit by small trios of red glass candle holders. The candlelight cast shadows against the brick walls.

In the far corner was a striking water feature that seemed both out of place, given the subterranean room, and also somehow perfect for the location. It was a bronze-cast fountain with three layers of bowls. The water trickled slowly from each layer down the next until it overflowed and fell into the round pool below. Faint lights underneath lit the fountain above in soft purples and blues. This was offset by several flame features crafted into center of the pool's lotus flowers. It appeared as if the water itself was on fire as the flames rose from the base of the lotus. Wagner imagined this was some kind of natural gas or propane effect. Even so, it was mesmerizing.

By far, the most prominent feature of the room was a long bar that ran the span of the right wall. The bar top was made of black Belgian marble and ornate wooden chairs with red leather upholstery lined it. There were two tall water containers on the top of either end of the bar. They were filled with ice and water and had four silver spouts set into the bottom of each. Wagner could make out the condensation on the outside of the glass. Cups of sugar cubes sat underneath the water dispensaries.  Several large elaborate silver spoons rested next to them.

The bar had the traditional three shelves of liquor and alcohol. The top shelf was filled with ornate bottles of expensive liquor. There were soft gold accent lights highlighting these choices. The middle line was filled with second-tier quality liquors. The well liquors ran along the bottom shelf. A female bartender was talking to a couple sitting on the left end of the bar.

Wagner realized he was standing in the entrance of the room like a cowboy in a spaghetti western. He imagined piano music stopping abruptly. He walked into the room and considered where to sit down. He noticed the man's eyes first. Deep set and ice blue, reminiscent of a Husky's eyes. The man sat back in his chair and laid his forearms on the old table with an expensive-looking tumbler resting between his hands. He stretched out his fingers and brought them back flat against the soft wood. His clothes matched the table, earth tones in his dusty linen shirt and faded blue jeans.

He gestured to Wagner to sit down across from him. Wagner sat. He extended his hand to the man at the table.

"Name's Dalton," the man said in a low, warm voice. He extended his hand and shook.

"Wagner. It's nice to meet you." He added, "Friends call me Wags."

"Wags. Got it. Need a drink?" Dalton asked in an off-handed way as his eyes drifted over to the bartender. He caught her eye quickly and Wagner was impressed by this; he had spent too many evenings trying to catch the attention of a bartender.

She came over with a smile and focused on Dalton. He lifted his almost empty glass. Ice clinked against the edge and the last remnants of the amber liquid sloshed across the bottom.

"Tess. This is my new friend, Wags." He turned his gaze to him, "What'll it be?"

Wagner looked at Tess. "Same as him, I think."

"Excellent," Dalton responded. "Two more, then."

"You got it." Tess flashed her smile to them and headed back to get the drinks.

"So, what brings you to this place?" Dalton finished the last of his drink and looked over to Tess as she poured two double shots of Johnny Walker Blue.

"That's quite a question. I wish I had a good answer to give you. I feel like I wandered here. Kind of drawn in. Though, I suppose that isn't a very good answer…" Wagner trailed off, rarely at a loss for words.

"Wandering," Dalton pondered. "I appreciate that more than you'd know. You could say that wandering has always been part of my life. I've seen so many different eyes and smiles—joy and pain." Dalton looked down briefly and then raised those deep blue eyes to meet Wagner's gaze.

Dalton said, "I think that's been one of my only constants. Ah well, doesn't do to talk it up too much, right? Talk the whole thing away."

Wagner looked surprised, "That's from one of my favorite Hemingway stories. I didn't think people read him much anymore."

Tess returned with the drinks and set them down between the two men. Dalton thanked her and asked her to add the drinks to his tab.

Dalton spoke, "I've spent my time on the road and books have been fair companions for me. I find they remind me of the Hindu concept of reincarnation, the idea of many lives. The more I read, the more I think I may move up the old reincarnation ladder."

"Get to where you are going a little faster?" Wagner asked.

Dalton smiled and offered a deep, resonate laugh. "Ha! That's exactly the thing." He nodded appreciatively. "No, I don't have anywhere I'm looking to be; I'm one of those 'it's about the journey, not the destination' kind of guys. You should come see my store, one of these times. I'm sure I would have something to interest you."

Wagner understood what Dalton was talking about. He had traveled to India and Nepal years ago. The trip had been a powerful one for him, but his one regret with it was how destination-driven it was. The guide pushed him, and there was something good in the physical exertion and the sights he saw from the mountain tops, but it left him wishing he had just slowed down. Took time to let the world pass him while resting on one of those sprawling green farms. Petting the neighborhood dog and getting to know the people in the villages he passed. The journey, not the destination, indeed.

Dalton said, "There was this group of early monks. The Ascetics. They believed that the pursuit of riches and the idea of structure—even the structure of the church—that all of these things took them away from truly knowing God. Like Thoreau in Walden Pond; even he eventually made a path for himself."

Wagner thought about this, finding himself agreeing again with the man. It reminded him of the idea that our vocation becomes a mask of sorts. Wagner had always found himself defined by his early work. He had taught English and creative writing at Emerson College in Boston. He had been tempted to chair the MFA in creative writing at one point, but the idea of vocation pulled him away from that. The more he wanted to be a writer, the more he was distracted from actually writing.

It had been profitable and comfortable for him, of course, and that was the seduction of it. We convince ourselves that our lives have meaning based on what we call ourselves. Assistant teacher, adjunct instructor, full professor, department chair. When, of course, none of those titles or honorariums amounted to anything. Just masks to keep the darkness at bay. Though, he supposed, masks of our own choosing.

Dalton shifted and Wagner noticed he seemed to pull at something on his left side. Dalton followed Wagner's gaze and smiled. "My little

Colt snub nose. Doesn't always stay were its supposed to stay; it was an anniversary gift from my first wife, Luanne. She didn't always stay where she was supposed to either."

Dalton took a long sip of his expensive scotch and continued, "Love of my life and she left me high and dry two months after our fifth anniversary for a marine biologist from Gulf Shores, Alabama."

He drank again, sad and instrospective. "It's like those lions on the beach. They have it figured out. You saw that picture coming in, right? There was something about those lions. Something in their eyes. Something in the way they watch the sea."

Wagner drank and watched Tess as she poured a deep glass of wine for the woman at the bar. The woman sat next to a fat man who nervously ran his hand through his thinning hair, talking incessantly.

"Alice, it's not all about the truth, you know?" the man said. He gestured to her glass and took a deep pull from his beer. "Bukowski will tell you. You need a special talent to be a drunk. It takes endurance. Endurance is more important than truth."

She looked at him sideways and rolled her eyes while taking a sip of her wine. She had been quite beautiful once and Wagner wondered why she was sitting here, what turn her life had taken to put her at the bar with that man.

"Harry," Alice said, "just drink your beer. Stop acting crazy."

"What?" Harry responded, "I'm just talking here. I don't know… hey! Hey!"

Wagner looked at them.

Harry gestured to Dalton and asked, "Dalton, what's your friend's name?" Harry waved at Wagner and said, "Hey there, new friend. I'm Harry. This here is Alice."

Dalton didn't speak and instead gestured to Wagner. Wagner spoke up, "I'm Wagner. It's nice to meet you…"

"Come settle something for us, Wagner. Come here for a moment," Harry said.

Wagner felt the pull of the room—Dalton in front of him sipping scotch and thinking about lions on the beach. Dalton nodded and gestured him to the bar with a wave of his hand. A subtle and nonchalant move. Easy and confident. Wagner liked the way Dalton carried himself. He had the air of someone well-traveled and wander-minded. Wagner reluctantly stood up and walked over to the bar.

Alice rested her hand against Wagner's shoulder and encouraged him to sit down. Part of her seemed to long for the company; whether that was a respite from Harry or an interest in him, Wagner wasn't sure.

Now that he was closer, he could tell that she was still attractive. Wagner always wondered about people who used to be very pretty. They approached the world with an expectation that people paid attention to them, laughed at their jokes, hung on their every word. And when their beauty faded, not by much mind you, but just enough to lose the intensity of it, they often became difficult to be around. Like a magician who couldn't quite move fast enough to pull off the illusion. The hang of a tenth of a second where the crowd saw the flash of the card in his sleeve.

Alice had that. The need to be the center of attention; trying to fill this deep sense of loss. Like it hadn't always been this way. It hadn't always been this hard for her. You could see the memory of it in her eyes. It was a mixture of sadness and confusion. Alice evoked the opposite feeling of what he had with Dalton. There was a disquiet about Alice. She was a glass resting too close to the edge of the table.

"Pull up a chair," Harry began. "I hate to advocate drugs and alcohol—or insanity—but they have always worked for me."

"Harry. Give him a break. And you're mixing your Bukowski with your Thompson," Alice added.

Harry looked down and mumbled something about bat country. He finished his beer and gestured to Tess for another.

Alice wore a soft blue dress accented with red flats. She had a dark blue velvet choker necklace that covered a portion of her neck. It had the effect of drawing attention to her delicately formed collar bones. Her legs were long and crossed. She wore a series of small silver bracelets on her left arm that gave off the faint glittering sound of bells as she gestured. It reminded Wagner of the soft movement of the prayer flags outside of Kathmandu. He had gone to Swayambhunath, the monkey temple, and climbed up to the top of it. The flags were tied to the trees and provided a background movement that was subtle; that was the way Alice's bracelets sounded. Her hand moved from Wagner's shoulder to a much more intimate resting place on his leg. Her eyes drew him in.

"This city. It speaks softly to those who listen. And you seem like someone who knows how to listen," she said.

Harry interrupted while scratching absentmindedly at the back of his head, "Listening. Yes. This is exactly the kind of thing we have been talking about. People don't know how to listen anymore. They watch things. Sure. They observe. But that isn't the same as really listening, you know? Really understanding."

Alice rolled her eyes again at Harry and sipped at her wine with a kind of unsteady grace that reflected her once beautiful features.

"It's the technology. I mean, there is no question about it. Everyone staring into these little boxes. Like something out of a badly-written sci-fi movie. All the people having their brains sucked out of their collective heads by the all-powerful god of 'what next.' That's the problem. Always looking for the next turn of the page. Like some goddamn Bob Seger song."

"Oh Harry. It's always the same with you. The same whining while you sit here drinking your beer and eating your pretzels. Just let it go and have another drink." She adjusted her choker and finished her glass of wine. She focused her attention back to Wagner. She trailed her fingers against his leg.

"Oh, you know I'm right, Alice. Vice is where the devil finds his darlings! You know I'm hitting the nail right on the head here. Dalton will tell you. He gets the mindfulness stuff. That uncarved block." Harry turned and shouted to Dalton, "No one stops to smell the goddamn roses anymore, am I right?" Dalton was momentarily lost in his thoughts but nodded back to Harry and said, "Ascetic wisdom…."

"Listen," Alice whispered to Wagner. "What do you say we get out of here, go find our own fun for a little bit?" She pulled at the choker with one hand, as if it suddenly was bothering her. Wagner wondered if that was to imply a desire to be out of her clothes.

"Will you excuse me for a moment? I'll be right back," Wagner said and asked Tess where the bathroom was. She gestured to the back of the bar. Wagner started to walk and then looked back. A small hole in her shirt like the one next to Landen's lapel. Was the place infested with moths? Wagner pondered and walked.

Alice looked disappointed as Wagner walked away. Harry didn't seem to notice and just took a long pull on his beer and continued to talk at Alice, "It's just that no one really takes the time to try to get to know each other anymore, you know? It wasn't always like this. Not really. People used to try to…"

The bathroom was in the back of the bar. Walking back, he noticed the music playing in the bar for the first time. It was some kind of bluegrass or Zydeco, turned down low.

The bar was unsettling. Wagner thought of a line from *Murder on the Orient Express*, "There is something about a tangle of strangers pressed together for days on end with nothing in common but the need to go from one place to another and then never to see each other again."

Wagner stepped up to the urinal and began to relieve himself. A whisper came from behind him and made him jump. Wagner looked back and saw no one. Just the music and the sound of his urine striking the porcelain. He finished and went to the sink to splash some water on his face. He had a strong feeling of vertigo. He walked unsteadily to the bathroom door and pushed it open.

He started to understand. It was like that moment when you remember a word that was on the tip of your tongue. On the outside of your memory. The déjà vu resolved. The girl. The white rabbit. He remembered it all and knew what was coming next.

The hairs on his arms came up and he felt sick. Overcome with that feeling you get when the roller coaster reaches its apex and, just for that small, small moment, it's all quiet before the fall begins. Sliding down the chute. There is an inevitability in what comes next.

From his vantage point at the back of the room, he saw himself sitting at the bar and then felt the sensation of falling backwards as his chair began a slow arc to the floor. The copper and wood ceiling unfolded in front of his vision like a 70s film low pan shot of an asphalt highway yellow line increasing speed until everything crashes loudly and fades to a brilliant white light. He felt the impact of his head on the floor as he watched himself come into hard contact with it.

Then the gunshots. He heard Alice as she screamed and Harry was silent, for once. The bullet caught Alice in her throat and the choker split cleanly in two and drifted to the floor. A haze of gun smoke filled the bar following the barrage of sharp pop, pop, pop sounds echoing in the small space. Wagner watched Harry as he turned to Alice. She clawed at the gaping red hole in her throat and started to fall from her bar stool. He tried to catch Alice before she fell. Wagner knew he wouldn't succeed.

The shot took Harry cleanly in the side of his head and he tumbled down on top of Alice, speeding her way to the wooden floor. Bright red arterial blood sprayed up across the bar and onto the collection of bottles on the shelves. Wagner watched as the metal horse from the top of the Blanton's bourbon bottle flew up. Bullets struck the bar as Tess ducked behind it, screaming.

Dalton pushed back his chair and stood while reaching down for the snub-nosed Colt .38 he kept in a side holster tight on his left waist. He kept it to protect his store and had drawn it twice before in his life; this would be the third time.

The first round of the Colt hit wide of its mark and sent chips of brick flying against the wooden floor. Wagner heard the quick succession of pop, pop, pop and the metallic sound of the rifle action chambering round after round as Dalton dropped Luanne's revolver to the floor, with five rounds unfired, as red stains spread across his blue shirt.

Tess continued to scream. Wagner watched himself scurry backwards, crab-like, on the floor. He remembered the disorientation and the nausea from when his head hit the floor. Her screams stopped suddenly as the pop, pop, pop sounds found her behind the bar.

The screaming echoed around his mind like the crackle and hum from speakers turned up too loud. The music had stopped but the reverberations still rang. Both Wagners closed their eyes and listened to the sound of steel-reinforced military boots cross the wood floor to where the shooter stood over the Wagner on the floor.

The terror from his nightmare. That recurring dream where the figure in the kitchen turned and looked at him.

From his position by the bathroom door, Wagner heard the voice. He knew the words it would say. He mouthed them as the man on the other end of the bar said "Well, I'll be goddamned. Isn't that some circular, serendipitous shit right here?"

The shooter paused and Wagner heard the click and slide of the magazine being taken from a rifle. The magazine struck the floor about four feet from where Floor Wagner was sprawled out.

"Wagner Sinclair, right? The writer?"

Floor Wagner kept his eyes closed and tried to convince himself this wasn't really happening. The other Wagner watched as the gunman reloaded the wicked looking bullpup rifle. He knew the rifle the shooter held. He knew the cape and wolf mask. He knew the shooter's name as well. It was Albert. It was an evil looking rifle with a military-grade red laser and a strobe flashlight on the opposite side that could be triggered by a touch pad next to the pistol grip. It was attached to him with a tactical holster. He also had a Glock pistol.

Wagner knew which company sold the armor piercing ammo. He also knew what version of the blue-tipped ammunition was currently loaded in Albert's rifle.

He knew it because he had written it.

"Of course you are. Of course." Albert laughed to himself. "Man, this is some Alanis Morissette level irony, right here."

The sound of Velcro being ripped apart filled the silence of the bar. This was followed by sliding plastic against nylon. The new magazine slapped into place with a loud metallic smack and the action of the rifle was pulled back.

Albert wore a black tactical load-bearing vest weighed down heavily with bullet proof plates on the chest and back. Several torn bits of fabric exposed the ceramic plates over his chest. The vest had done its job well, however, and none of the rounds had penetrated.

Now, with a fresh 50-round clip in place, he smiled, pleased with himself. He took his mask off so he could speak more clearly, "Do you know this joke? A man with a gun walks into a bar." Floor Wagner scurried backwards, trying to get away from the danger.

Albert continued, "This man comes into a bar with the gun. He waves the gun around like some kind of crazy person. He's pointing it at all the other men in the bar. He has these eyes, right? These wild animal eyes. You know he has been through some shit. So, there he is, waving the gun around and…you know what's coming, right? Right? Then he yells out 'Which one of you slept with my wife?!?'"

Floor Wagner backed into the corner. He saw Dalton's body slowly bleeding out next to him. The colt .38 lay just a few feet away from Dalton's dead hand. Maybe…

Albert turned on the red laser site. Even with all the gun smoke in the bar, the laser was bright and pierced the space between the shooter and Wagner.

The other Wagner watching this from the doorway wanted to scream. He wanted to tell his doppelganger to stop listening, to get the Colt. To put all five rounds in this psychopath's twisted head.

Albert continued with the joke, "And from somewhere in the crowd... Hey!" Albert saw that Wagner wasn't listening. "Listen up, this is the best part. Don't miss this. From somewhere in the crowd, this guy yells back, 'Buddy! You ain't got enough bullets!'"

The red light jumped around on Floor Wagner until Albert was right above him. He said with a sly smile, "Not enough bullets. Har Har. Cause that sneaky snatch BITCH was a straight-up, goddamn whore. You get it? A goddamn whore. She had fucked the whole bar, she was such a slut. Poor dumb bastard."

Albert breathed deeply and then stopped laughing. He said, "Mr. Wagner fucking Sinclair. Unbelievable. And they say there isn't a god. Stare into the abyss long enough…"

Floor Wagner brought his gaze to the shooter and forgot all about the snub-nosed Colt a few feet from him. He looked him right in the eyes.

Wagner held the door jam and tried to steady himself. The next words he knew well. They were the end to…

Where the vest had been shot through and where the panel was torn open, Floor Wagner saw the fox on the shirt. And he knew what else the t-shirt said. It said, "I don't give a fox." Except where the word fox was, it was a picture of the fox. Then the Wagner on the floor knew what the other Wagner knew.

"Albert. How can this be… You are…" Wagner stammered.

"Stare into the abyss long enough, Mr. Sinclair, and that abyss stares back into you…"

The rounds hit Wagner's chest and his breath left him, along with his life.

A rushing noise filled the bar. Like someone had turned on a wind tunnel. Turned that wind tunnel all the way up to 11 and broke off the knob. The remaining Wagner felt like Dorothy in the tornado. The world spun and the bar faded away. In the background, he heard something faint. The hazy strumming of a guitar player. He was singing Bob Dylan's classic, "Tangled up in Blue."

And then Wagner felt everything slipping away again.

His thoughts and memories faded.

And it began again.

www.ingramcontent.com/pod-product-compliance
Lightning Source LLC
Chambersburg PA
CBHW061122100726
47911CB00013B/643